Step Softly; Ere You Go
A Matt Murphy Mystery #1

H. Paul Doucette

Print ISBNs
Amazon print 9780228627616
Ingram Spark 9780228627623
BWL Print 9780228627630

Table of Contents

Chapter One

The small studio was cloaked in semi-darkness, except for the stream of moonlight coming through the skylight; some of the light spilling over the polished hard wood floor. A large full length mirror, with a long hand rail attached to it, filled one entire wall. There was a baby grand piano sitting in one corner. The room had an almost ethereal feel which, to one attuned to such things, seemed to have faint echoes of dreams and hopes emanating from the old wooden walls.

The young woman dressed in black clothing, quietly walked across the open area to the door that led to the locker rooms on the other side. She opened the door and passed through, closing the door behind her. Taking out a flashlight, she made her way to the dressing rooms and, finding the one she was looking for, opened the door and went in. Going directly to a locker, she opened it and extracted a pair of well worn pointe shoes, ballet slippers, then went to the small make-up table and sat down, setting the shoes on the table.

She reached inside the pocket of her coat and pulled out a small cardboard box, about the size of a box of matches. She opened it and carefully took out three sewing needles that had been nipped in half and began to insert them into the toes of each shoe with the pin points protruding just enough to ensure they broke the skin but not so much as to cause permanent damage.

Once she was satisfied with her work, she returned the shoes to the locker then, after a quick look around, left the room and headed out of the studio.

* * *

It was one of those really great spring days, you know the ones, filled with the promise of the coming summer that lay just around the corner with its heat rising from baked pavement trapped between the buildings. Until then, warm air gently blew in the open window behind my desk carrying with it the smells and sounds of the Village: an old familiar melody I never grew tired of hearing.

My name is Matt Murphy. I run a one man detective agency with my girl Friday, Maddie Cox, out of a small office on Belmuto Street, not far from the Village. I know what you're thinking; a private eye, wow. Late nights in smoke filled bars rubbing elbows with wise guys, hoods, loose dames, a cigarette in the corner of my mouth and a glass of whiskey, straight up of course, with a look of menace and disdain on my face. Not even close.

My main business comes from a couple of insurance companies that have me on retainer to look into certain claims. I also work for two law firms on a regular basis when they need background or alibi checks done. The riskiest work I do is when some visiting 'somebody' visits the Village and needs protection. These assignments come in from a contact, Saul Rubinek, a theatrical agent, who needs someone like me to play babysitter. It isn't the most glamorous work, but it pays the bills and puts something in the bank. I almost never have to use my gun.

I recently married the long time love of my life, Jane Caldwell, and live in a cozy flat in a quaint one bedroom renovated Victorian house on Bellair Street just down from Critchley and Bloor. It is owned by an equally old, but motherly widow, who thinks I should get a real job. She dotes on Jane like she was her daughter, which is okay with me.

I love Yorkville Village and have done so since I first came to Toronto from Manitoba back in '54. By day, it's like any other place; people going about their daily lives; working, eating, making love; the usual stuff. But after dark! Now, that's when it awakens with its clubs and bars and the streets crawling with gawkers, thrill seekers, music lovers and nowadays, hippies, dopers, and runaways, all searching for...whatever. The papers compare it to Greenwich Village in New York and Haight-Ashbury in San Francisco; three pillars of what they call the counterculture movement.

On this particular day, Friday to be exact, I was happy to just sit back and enjoy the day thinking about the love of my life.

I was sitting in my office with my feet up on the corner of the desk listening to a song on the radio by a couple of kids named Simon and Garfunkel. They sang well together with really nice harmonies.

Most of the news in the Globe and Mail seemed to be focused on the tensions between the Soviets and the U.S.; the States' growing involvement in a place called Vietnam and the situation in Cuba. I couldn't help wondering why they felt the need to become involved in the affairs of other countries, especially ones where there didn't seem to be any apparent economic interests. I mean, didn't they have enough going on right here at home with the growing unrest and protests.

I wasn't looking to take on any new cases for a while anyway, but as usual, the gods who appear to have taken an interest in my life had other ideas. I'm not a religious man, but I sometimes think someone or something out there has singled me out for attention, or maybe it's just karma. Either that, or they were bored up there on their mountain and they chose today to have some fun.

It had been over six months since my last big case. That one involved my best friend, Abe Goldman, who is a detective on the Metropolitan Police Force. He was working with the drug squad on an undercover operation in the Village and at Rochdale College. The case turned sour, and he got shot by a member of a bike gang that ran the trade out of the College. Luckily he survived. The shooter was never caught. The police eventually put their investigation on the back burner for the obvious reasons. So, I set out to find who was behind it. Friendship matters, especially with me.

Turned out to be a couple of dirty cops.

Abe recovered and was now back on the job where he got promoted to Lieutenant and re-assigned to Internal Affairs at headquarters downtown.

As I was saying, the gods decided that I must have been idle long enough, so, in their wisdom and to make sure I didn't slip into an easy comfortable life, they sent her to my door.

"Mr. Murphy?" she said, knocking softly on the glass panel, as she opened the door. Maddie must have stepped away from her sentry post: the reception desk.

"That's me," I said, swinging my feet to the floor and swiveling the chair to face her.

She stood about five-six. Looked to be in her forties. A nice looking slender figure with long legs. It all came wrapped in a colorful floral dress that hung down to just above her knees. She wore a light woolen waist length jacket. Her thick red hair was tied up in a bun at the back of her head but didn't have that severe matronly look you'd expect. Not many women could have pulled off that look as well as she did. She wore just enough makeup to accent her facial features perfectly. By anyone's standard she was a looker.

"Have a seat, uh..."

"Adele Smithson," she said, as she moved gracefully and sat in one of the two chairs in front of the desk.

"Okay," I said. "How can I help you?"

"I've come to you on the recommendation of Saul Rubinek. He said you're the detective that was involved in that horrible business with those poor actors some time ago. Is that correct?"

"Yes," I said. Uh-oh, was that the sounds of chuckling from above.

"Good, then I have come to the right man." She settled back into the chair, relaxing her shoulders. "I own a dance studio on Isabella Street, across from George Hisop Park. It's not a very big studio as such, but I have several of the more notable dancers in the city in my company. Are you familiar with the dance scene?"

"Not really. I have seen a few performances but that's it."

"Yes. I see. Well, as I was saying, I have a studio. At the present time, it consists of twelve permanent dancers and a list of a dozen or so call ups."

I must have given her a funny look at that point because she said, "Call ups are dancers who are not a permanent part of any company but who are available as extras, stand-ins, that sort of thing."

"Ah, thanks," I said. "Go on."

She nodded and continued, "For the last two months we have been in rehearsal for the debut a new production by one of the most promising new choreographers to come along in the last ten years." She paused waiting for a response from me. When none came she continued.

"Yes, well, suffice it to say, there is a lot of interest in his work. Because of the importance of this production, we have received a number of offers from some of the major dancers in the city, and from abroad, to lead the performance. However, the choreographer has indicated that he has a girl in mind for the lead. She's a young dancer from Montreal that he met while directing another dance there and was greatly impressed with her. Of course, I agreed with his request. After all, this is a major event, and I'm honored that he chose my company to debut it in this country." She paused for a moment.

"Uh-huh," I said, "guess you would be. So why do you need the services of a private investigator?"

"I recently visited Montreal to meet this girl and to see her dance. Her name is Monique Levesque. I was quite impressed. She is a natural, and quite nice as well. I invited her to come to Toronto which she accepted. That was two weeks ago. The production has a two week run here before going on tour. Opening night is scheduled for three weeks from now. She has been in rehearsals during this time."

She took a moment before continuing. I took this opportunity to offer her a coffee, which she accepted. I got up, poured a cup and placed it on the desk in front of her, then sat back down.

"Thank you. As I was saying, during this time a number of, ah, things have happened."

"Things? What kind of things?" I asked, taking a few notes as she told her story.

"Odd things, I guess you'd say. Nothing dramatic or suspicious as such. It's just that, taken individually, one would think they were nothing more than little accidents, you know, the kind that happen in a studio. It's just that there have been enough for me to wonder, you see. It just seems to me to be stretching coincidence to keep thinking these are just a series of accidents."

"Can you tell me what exactly has happened?"

"Props falling. Exercise bars coming loose, those kind of things. But it was something that happened two days ago.

When Monique arrived for rehearsal she discovered that there were several pins embedded in the toe of her practice shoes. Which is why I have come to you."

"And that's serious because...," I asked, sounding a little puzzled.

"Because of the potential damage it could cause to a ballet dancer. It could, at the worst, ruin or end her career."

"Gotcha. Sorry. Has there been anything else as threatening happening to her or any of the other dancers?"

"No. My God, you make it sound like someone is deliberately doing these things."

"Well, you have to ask yourself how the pins got there. Somebody had to have done it," I said.

"Oh," she said, looking upset at the prospect, as if she hadn't considered that before.

"I assume that other studios were in competition for this deal, if so, do you think any of them might harbor some resentment against yours for being chosen?"

"It is a competitive world, yes, but to actually do something to endanger a dancer...I can't believe that. Not many understand the nuances within the dance community, but this? No. There has to be another reason."

"Uh-huh. However, from what you've given me so far, it sounds like someone isn't happy that you won the deal."

"Are you suggesting there may be someone trying to harm the girl or maybe sabotage the production?"

I nodded.

"It's a possibility, yes, although, for the life of me, I can't imagine who would do such a thing." She sat with a worried look on her face. It was obvious that the possibility was upsetting her.

After a moment, she said, "If what you are suggesting is even remotely true then it seems that I really do need your services. So, can you help me?"

"Yeah. I don't see a problem. I have nothing pressing at this time."

"Wonderful. You do understand that this will require a certain degree of, ah, discretion," she said, with a slight smile. "The last thing I need is for any negative or adverse publicity to..."

"Not to worry," I said, interrupting her. "I understand."

"Good," she said. "I had hoped that I could rely on your understanding of the situation."

I outlined how I would proceed.

I would show up at the studio and nose around a little. I also wanted to be able to talk to her dancers, including the Levesque girl. We agreed that I would pose as a freelance reporter doing a feature story on her company and the upcoming performance. That should avoid any concerns as well as putting the dancers at ease. She agreed to my plan without any fuss and even agreed to a two hundred dollar retainer.

I made a few calls to my regular clients after she left to let them know I wouldn't be available for the next couple of weeks. That wasn't an issue. I had a good working relationship with another detective who covered for me when I needed him. Before leaving I called one of my favorite clubs and made reservations for dinner, then called Jane.

Chapter Two

It was a beautiful Sunday morning. The sun was shining, the air pleasantly fresh and clear. I was lounging on my sofa with the weekend paper and a cup of fresh brewed coffee, enjoying the smell of frying bacon coming from the small kitchen as Jane made breakfast.

We've been together for more than two years. Right from the beginning, she accepted what I did for a living and who I am as a man. There were times that tried her, especially whenever I took a case that carried some degree of danger, but she still held on. She worried, of course, but never said anything or complained. I promised myself I would never give her cause to worry, if possible. In time, I grew to the realization that we loved each other.

Our relationship grew closer and deeper. so one day while on one of our favorites walks, I asked her to marry me. She accepted without batting an eye. That was six months ago, now we live together, agreeing it made more sense for me to move into her apartment on Bellair Street not far from Critchley. It was close to Queen's University where she worked as a researcher in the library.

I looked over the top of the paper and marveled at her beauty as I always do.

She stood bare foot at the stove wearing nothing but one of my shirts and an apron; the shirt was three sizes too big but she still looked better in it than I ever could. My eyes traveled over her one hundred and fifteen pound, five-foot-four, slender body with a tapered waist and perfectly rounded hips and beautiful legs. Her hair was thick and black; kept at shoulder length, which this morning was tied off in a short ponytail. I could just make out the soft outline of her firm round buttocks beneath the shirt.

I wondered how the bacon would taste cold.

"Stop that," she said, without turning around.

"Huh? Stop what?" I said, snapping out of my reverie.

"You know. Is that all you ever think about?" she said with a soft chuckle.

"Is that a complaint" I asked.

"Let's eat first. You need to keep your energy up...among other things."

"I knew there was a good reason why I married you."

I dropped the paper to the floor then got up and went to the table.

"The only reason?"

"Well... not only. Let's eat. I just realized I'm hungry."

"You're always hungry, you," she said, giggling. "So am I. C'mon. It's ready."

She placed two plates filled with bacon and eggs on the table. There was a plate with four slices of buttered toast already there. Maddie sat on the wooden chair to my left,

"Tell me more about this new job you've taken?"

"Nothing to tell, really. I'm to look into some strange things that have been happening at this woman's dance studio, especially those that seem to happening around a new dancer; a girl from Montreal."

"Uh-huh. What's she like?"

"Who? The dancer?"

"Uh-huh," she said, taking a bite of her toast. Women, I thought. Why is it they always want to know about any other woman that comes along.

"Not much yet. She's from Montreal, young and a dancer. This is supposed to be her first time to Toronto," I said with a shrug.

"Sounds like an easy job."

I saw the look that came into her eyes. "This should be a cake walk; what's the worst that could happen...they start to kick each other to death with those shoes they wear? So, try not to worry."

"It's just that I always get a little twinge in my stomach whenever you take on a new job."

"I know. Like I said, what's the worst that could happen with a high strung dancer? Nothing I can't handle, right?"

"I know that, it's...," she started to say.

"So. Whaddya wanna do today?" I asked, quickly changing the subject.

She sat quietly for a moment then said, "I thought we might give Millie and Abe a call and get away for the day somewhere."

"Sounds great. Anyplace in particular?"

"How about over to Kensington Market? You know, we could check out the stalls then maybe go to dinner and then a show at the Riverboat. I hear Gordon Lightfoot is in town," she said. Or we could head down to T's and see who' playing."

"Yeah, sounds good. Especially the part about T's. We could even do dinner there. You know how much I like T's cookin'.

"Oh, yes," she said. "Let's do that."

"I'll call them after we eat."

"Not right after we eat..." she said, giggling.

"Oh, yeah...right after that," I said with a smile.

"I love you," she said.

"And why wouldn't you," I said, grinning like a love struck teenager.

"Oh you." She laughed.

We finished eating and I helped with the clean up.

"Now," I said, "I think it's 'bout time I had a talk with you about wearing my shirts..."

I followed her down the hallway as she skipped to our bedroom.

When we decided to get married we agreed that I would try and not take on any more dangerous cases where I would be at risk of being killed. It was not that hard to agree to, because in point of fact, I was never really interested in that side of the business.

In the past, such cases generally only turned out that way well into the job. Besides, I was crouching up into my middle forties and did not need the aggravation. Don't get me wrong, I'm still in pretty good shape. I keep up with my boxing three or four days a week. So, I can handle myself in a pinch, but one thing life has taught me is that no matter how good you think you are, there will always be someone better or more dangerous around the corner. Besides, the most important lesson I've learned from boxing is that almost always when you hit someone they hit back, and I have recently acquired an allergy to pain.

I mentioned this epiphany to Abe recently; his only response was, 'Uh-huh'. Sardonic bastard.

Abe and Millie. Probably the only other couple as much into each other as Jane and me. He met Millie Wainwright while he was in recovery after he was shot. They hit it off immediately and since he was single again after his wife left him, they started a relationship. Six months lather, a week after Jane and I got married, they decided to move in together. Turned out to be one of his better decisions.

Millie is a great gal. We first met when she hired me to work on her divorce a couple of years ago. When Abe and Phyllis, his long time wife, decided to call it quits, I introduced him to Millie. Turned out to be the best thing to happen to both of them. Since then, Jane and Millie have become really close friends, spending quite a bit of time together doing whatever girls do. So, when I called, it didn't take any time at all to set up the weekend. It was agreed that we would take my car and that we would pick them up around noon.

* * *

Monday arrived bright with clear skies. Always a good way to start one's day.

We left the apartment and went downstairs to my car. Jane got in on the passenger's side. After dropping her off at the Queen's University Library where she worked in the Special Collections Department with a promise to call later, I headed to the dance studio over on Isabella Street.

I arrived at nine-forty-five and, after finding a parking spot, entered the studio's reception area. It was located on the second floor above a ladies clothing store. The only person there was the receptionist; a middle aged woman who looked like she might have been a dancer at some time in her life. After telling her who I was, she escorted through a door into a hallway with an office at the far end. I could hear a piano playing on the other side of the only other door. I assumed that was the studio. She deposited me on a comfortable chair and said I was to wait for Miss Smithson who was busy in the studio at the moment.

Adele Smithson emerged at ten sharp.

Today, she was wearing a tailored and stylish light gray pantsuit with a pale pink blouse, open at the neck. Her hair, which was shoulder length, was down this time with a pair of ornate combs on either side. Very fetching, very fetching indeed, I thought.

She spotted me and came over. I noticed for the first time that she moved with an economy of motion and the definite grace of a dancer.

"Good morning Mr. Murphy. I hope you had an enjoyable weekend," she said, offering her hand which I accepted as I stood up.

"Miss Smithson," I said. "Please, call me Murph, everyone does and yes, I did, in fact. Thanks for asking."

"Adele. I suppose you would like to get started. Where would you like to begin?"

"Maybe a quick walk through the studio before it gets busy," I said. Once we were out of earshot of the receptionist, I added, "Can you show where some of these accidents happened?"

"Of course, over here," she said, as she led me into a large room. The floor was polished hardwood and reflected the bright overhead lights which were on despite the flood of light from the bank of high windows along the length of one side. The only furnishing was a baby grand piano in one corner. I spotted a horizontal bar that was attached to a bank of mirrors that filled one wall.

"This is the part that was loose." She pointed to the area where a bracket attached to the bar was screwed into the wall at the seam of two mirror panels.

"And what exactly made you suspicious?" I bent slightly to look at the bracket.

"The screws were, well, loosened enough so that if enough pressure was brought to bear it would have suddenly come away from the wall. If someone was stretching at the time, they could have injured themselves."

"Hmm. Tell me, is this where Levesque exercises? Or does she work out elsewhere?" I asked, looking around the large wooden floored room.

"Funny you should ask. Yes, this is where she frequently comes to stretch. I hadn't thought of that." We stood for a moment while I scanned the room.

"The other incidents happened around the studio area," she said, with a sweep of her arm.

Just at that moment Monique Levesque arrived.

She was a vision of youthful beauty. Long dark hair tied off with a red silk scarf in the back. She stood around five-six or so with the typlical slender ballerina figure. She wore black leotards beneath a pale blue skirt and a white Angora shrug sweater. There was a jacket draped over her arm and a kit bag slung over one shoulder. As she walked into the room, I immediately noted her legs. Long with toned muscles that looked sculpted and strong. There was no mistaking her for anything other than a ballet dancer.

"And this is Mademoiselle Monique Levesque, our lead dancer for the upcoming performance," Adele said, as the girl came toward us.

"Hi," I said, offering her my most charming smile. She rewarded me with an equally charming smile.

"Mr. Murphy is a freelance writer who is doing a feature piece on the studio and the performance. He will be visiting with us for the next several days as he gathers his background information. I hope that you will be cooperative and help him with his efforts," Adele said.

"But, of course," Monique said with a warm smile.

"Wonderful. Now if you'll excuse me, I have a studio to run." Adele turned and walked away leaving just the two of us.

"Who do you write for, Mr. Murphy?" she asked, with a faint trace of a French accent, as she dropped her kit bag to the floor and sat down. She dug out a pair of well worn dance slippers and started to put them on.

"I work freelance. You know, write an article then sell it to whoever's interested."

"Are you a follower of dance?" She rose gracefully and started to limber up, pulling one outstretched leg up, placing her ankle on the bar then slowly bending forward touching her forehead to her knee. I realized as I watched her that even exercising was sensuous. I got the definite impression she was teasing me...if she was, it was working.

"Not really. That's the nice thing about freelance. I get to do a whole lot of different stories. Learn a lot more that way."

"Mmm, you look like you know a lot, that's for sure," she said with a smile.

Definitely teasing. I decided to change the subject.

"I thought dancers always wore those flat-toed shoes?" I asked, noting that she was wearing a pair of slip-on slippers.

"They are called, pointe shoes. And yes, we do wear them, but usually when we are performing or need to practice a particular part."

"Oh. I see."

Just then, I heard the sounds of giggling and laughter, as several young men and women entered the room. They glanced my way for a brief moment then went on with their preparations for the class. I excused myself and went for walk around the back areas to do a little 'detecting'. After all, that's what I was being paid to do.

Besides the main dance area that I just left, there were three smaller rooms which were used as classrooms for new students. Down near the back, I located two small changing rooms with a toilet in each; one for men, the other, women. The last place I looked at seemed to be a general storage area where various props were kept in no particular order. Anyone could access the area.

Music was coming from one of the rooms and I assumed that a class was beginning somewhere. There wasn't much else to see, so I went looking for Smithson.

She was in her office going over some papers. The room was quite small with only a desk, two straight back wooden chairs and a four drawer file cabinet in a corner. There was one window in the wall directly behind her chair.

"Spare a few minutes?" I asked, as I tapped the glass panel in the door that was already open.

"Certainly. Please," she said, gesturing to one of the chairs. "Did you see everything you needed?"

"Pretty much. It looks like a pretty compact studio. How many students do you actually have here?" I asked, as I closed the door and sat down.

"We offer six classes. Three beginners, two intermediate and one advanced. The classes are small, usually around twelve per class. Of course, there is also the permanent company which I already indicated."

"And does this group meet every day?"

"Not usually, no. They come here mostly to practice for a scheduled performance. Normally, only a few at a time, unless it's a major production like this one involving the entire company."

"I see. Do you happen to keep files on the members? You know, addresses and any background information?"

"Yes, of course. Why do you ask?"

"I was hoping that you would allow me to give them a quick look."

"I don't see the relevance, but if you really feel it's necessary...," she said, giving me a questioning look.

"Assuming that the things that have been happening are not simply accidents, the only other explanation is that someone is behind them. For the purposes of my investigation, I'm going to go on the assumption that these are not accidents. Better to start from the worst situation and eliminate it than to ignore it and pay a price later. Therefore, I need to know something about all the people involved."

"Yes, I see. All the company member files are in the bottom drawer. When would you like to review them?"

"Preferably when there is no one around."

"That would be after ten in the evening or early in the morning, before the studio opens at nine."

"If it's okay with you, I think I'll come by after the studio closes."

"Here is a spare key to the building and the studio," she said, as she opened a desk drawer and pulled out a set of two keys on a small chain.

I accepted the keys and put them in my pocket, saying thanks as I did.

"When do plan to come around?" she asked, as I stood up.

"Either tonight or tomorrow. I'll return the keys once I've finished and report anything I come across."

"That'll be fine, thank you."

"Right then. I'll take off for now and see you later. There are a few things I want to look into." She gave me another questioning look.

"Background." This answer seemed to satisfy her.

I left after another quick peek into the main dance room. Monique was still in her corner but was now doing some stretches without the bar. Other dancers were in various stages of warming up while an older looking man with a tall staff stood beside a baby grand piano discussing something with the pianist.

Chapter Three

I left the studio and made my way down to the theatre district. It was time to talk to Saul Rubinek; first to thank him for the referral and, second, to pick his brain about the dance community. His theatrical agency office was located down in the theatre district. He has been a fixture in the theatre community for quite a long time and had represented a number of notable luminaries of the stage.

We met a couple of years ago when he engaged me to baby-sit some star that was visiting the city from New York. Apparently, this person had a bit of a 'bad boy' reputation and was frequently in trouble. Anyway, after three days, the actor returned to the States and Saul was more than satisfied with my handling of the assignment; he even gave me a hundred dollar bonus.

I dropped my car back at the office, opting to take the subway, because parking downtown was a hassle and a real pain in the ass these days. I didn't need the aggravation or the expense. I had called ahead and made an appointment for two o'clock, so I was expected. This gave me a bit of time to stop and pick up a box of fairly good cigars as a thank you gift. Saul's only vice these days was his passion for a good cigar.

I arrived at one fifty and found his assistant, Isobel, sitting at her guard post; a medium sized desk just to the right of his office door. She hadn't changed much since I last saw her over a year ago. Still had her trademark stern matronly look going, although, she was sporting new glasses. No one, small or great and famous, got past her without an appointment. She would give you a look that could stop a charging elephant if you dared to try.

There were several men and women sitting around the room waiting their turn with the man hoping to solicit his representation. I went and stood in front of her desk and waited for her to look up.

"Mr. Murphy. Nice to see you again," she said, without a smile. I wondered if she ever smiled. "You are eight minutes early."

"Isobel," I said, flashing my best award winning smile. Nothing. Not even a crack. The woman must be made of stone. I felt deflated.

"Take a seat. He'll be free momentarily," she said, gesturing to the few vacant chairs against the wall.

"Thank you," I said, as I retreated from the cold atmosphere at the desk and sat down.

Five minutes later, the door behind her opened and a pretty young woman stepped out wearing a broad smile. Rubinek stood behind her. She turned and shook his hand and said thank you. Must've scored. Good for her. Then he spotted me over her shoulder.

"Ah, Mathew, my boy. Please, please come in. How good to see you again."

He was one of three people in my life that ever called me Mathew. The young woman gave me a curious look, trying to decide if I was someone important, as she stepped past me to the door. I gave her a smile as I walked by.

"Saul," I said. We had agreed some time ago to drop the formalities.

"Please," he said, as I stepped into his office.

"Thanks."

Saul Rubinek was a heavily built Jewish man in his mid-sixties with thinning white hair and a friendly looking face above a jowl that sagged beneath his cheeks. He was dressed, as always, in a dark blue three piece pin-striped suit with a gold watch chain hanging across the front of the vest.

He closed the door behind me and moved back behind his desk, gesturing me to sit in one of the chairs in front of it.

"That what I hope it is?" he said, pointing at the bag in my hand as he sat down.

"Yep," I said, passing the plain brown bag across to him. "A small thanks for the referral."

"You are such a considerate 'goy'," he said, smiling. "Thank you. Completely unnecessary, but I thank you all the same. It's the only vice I still can enjoy. Now. What can I do for you?" he asked, as he opened the box and extracted a cigar. He rolled it between his fingers then moved it across his upper lip under his nose with his eyes closed.

"Would you mind," he asked, reaching for his lighter.

"Help yourself. Don't do much good sitting in the box."

"Quite so." He flashed up the cigar and a cloud of light blue smoke rose lazily above him.

"Thank you, my boy. You are one of only a few that thinks of me." He had a warm wide smile on his face as he took the bag and slipped it into a drawer in his desk.

"Let me guess, Adele Smithson," he said. "Can I offer you something?"

"No thanks, and yes, Miss Smithson. She has filled me in on her concern. So far, all I've been able to find out is her studio seems to be the victim of a series of, uh, nuisance incidents. I'm not sure what I can do. Perhaps, if I had a better understanding of that world, I'd have a better chance to see if there's something more sinister going on. You're the only one I know who might be able to give me a quick education, you know, Ballet 101."

"I see. Well, as you may recall, my stock in trade is predominantly the theatre.

However, I do take an interest in other aspects of the performing arts; music, dance, that sort of thing, although not an active role. Mostly, I am in the background more as a donor or patron, sometimes as a facilitator in bringing the right people together, if you follow me."

I nodded. As I mentioned before, he was a well known figure in the arts community.

"Well, about a year ago I met her during a small production she staged at one of the local venues and was very impressed with her dancers. We struck up a conversation and from that time on I have been involved with her studio as a silent partner. So, when she came to me with her recent concerns and their possible effects on an upcoming production, I immediately thought of you. After all, you do seem to have a broad interest and appreciation for this part of Village life."

"Thanks. Just how much is going on in the Village these days with dance? I mean, I've seen several posters for shows but it didn't strike me as that prominent."

"Oh, it's definitely here and growing. Mostly, it seems to be small troupes, usually around a half dozen or so young dancers in each, that have been running the circuit of clubs and playhouses. The main interest tends toward the new avant-garde movement, more free expression and less traditional ballet. Interesting ideas."

"Is there much competition between these different groups? You know, one style over another? For performing places?"

"Interesting question. I wouldn't have considered that, but I suppose there would be some competition to a degree but no more than already exists within the community in general."

"Well, if her suspicions are correct, then I think someone out there has decided to go a few steps beyond the normal practices."

"Hmm. I see your point. However, from my understanding of the dance world, I think it highly unlikely that this would be coming from the modern groups. They're just so different in their philosophy and artistic motivations. There doesn't seem to be anything to gain from such actions."

"Then that leaves rival traditional ballets groups who might see this new movement as a threat to their own productions. And if it's someone from there, then what would be their motive."

"It seems to me that if you're looking for a motive then maybe you might consider the upcoming production."

"Yeah. I was thinking the same thing. I get the impression that this is a big deal. Maybe someone out there resents Adele's studio getting the chance to debut this new guy's work."

"It's a possibility, yes. I hope not, but it is a competitive world and regrettably, the arts are no longer immune to the vagaries of profits and losses. Art has become a commodity, an avenue of investment, and as such, it has to pay those who fund it. And, yes, this is a significant venture with the opportunity for substantial financial rewards as well as opening doors for future opportunities."

"So, maybe someone feels short changed and is upset enough to strike back," I said.

"Hmm," Rubinek said, flicking an inch long ash from the cigar into the ashtray.

"A thought just occurred to me," I said.

"Yes?"

"Is it possible that this business could be as simple as another dancer seeking to strike back at the dancer who was given the lead? One from outside, like Monique Levesque?"

"Interesting," Saul said, leaning forward on his forearms. "Dancers, even more than actors, have very delicate sensibilities which are easily bruised."

"It was just a thought. What can you tell me about this choreographer?"

He spent the next ten minutes filling me in on the choreographer, Pierre St. Jacques. When he finished I had a better idea of what I was getting into. It was clear that whoever was chosen to be the lead dancer for any St. Jacques production would have some very serious career opportunities open up to them.

Maybe I might have just found a loose end to pull on.

After leaving Rubinek's office, I decided to head over to see Abe Goldman.

We have a long history together dating back to when we both entered the police academy in 1954. I was a new kid in from Manitoba, and he, from one of the north Ontario towns, Barrie. Unfortunately, it didn't take with me, but Abe took to it like a duck to water. Later, after several years moving from job to job and a stint in the merchant marine on a laker, I came back, and we reconnected.

He had been assigned to a station up in the Yorkville area by then. It did not take me long to discover I liked the feel of the place as well, so I settled in. The only skill and training I had for work ashore was police work, but I didn't want to wear the blue uniform again, so I got a P.I. License with a carry endorsement and hung out my shingle.

I arrived at the station around the time for the shift change. I knew he'd still be there finishing the day's paperwork. I went straight to the second floor where the Homicide Squad had their room.

"Hey Gus. What's shakin'?" I said, offering my hand to the detective bent over a file. Gus Ferguson was a friend and a good cop. We helped each other on a couple of cases I worked over the last few years.

"Murph," he said, sitting back accepting my extended hand. "Same old shit only more of it. You'?"

"Nothing much really. Just thought I'd stop by and see Abe. Take him for a beer. You can come to, if you're free."

"Thanks, but I gotta get this crap cleared up. You know the routine."

"Yeah, I know," I said. "Is he in?"

"Yeah. Go ahead." He leaned forward and went back to work.

"Yeah?" Abe called from behind the closed door after I knocked.

I opened the door and went in. "Hey, buddy. Thought I'd buy you a beer. Interested?"

"Hell, yeah. This desk work sucks. I don't know what I hate more, paperwork or dirty cops. Days like this I miss the streets."

"Really?"

"Really. But then I remember what the streets are like these days."

"Uh-huh," I said.

He started closing files and stacking them on the corner of his desk then stood up and reached for his hat.

"Let's go before I change my mind," he said. I'm calling it a day, Gus. If you need anything from the Morgan case file, it's sitting on my desk, top of the pile."

"Okay, thanks. See ya guys later," Gus said, looking back at the papers in front of him.

"Yeah. Tomorrow."

We headed out of the building and walked the block and a half to Benny's, the local bar. The establishment was where the cops hung out after their shifts before heading home. It was a typical neighborhood bar like dozens of others...must be a universal design.

An old wooden topped bar with eight stools fronting it and five booths along the opposite side. There was a large mirror on the wall behind the bar partly covered down one side with glued on shoulder patches from a variety of police organizations like the OPP – Ontario Provincial Police – and the RCMP – the Royal Canadian Mounted police. On the other wall were a couple of dozen framed photographs of former cops from the area's station. Many of them now long dead or retired.

There were also a couple with serving members including one of Mike Clark with a couple of uniforms around him. Mike was once an instructor at the academy when I was there and now Abe's boss, a real hard nose but fair and a good cop and friend.

We went to the bar and took a couple of stools.

"Still don't like the desk job, I take it?" I said, as Mickey, the bartender placed two tall glasses of Budweiser drafts in front of us.

"Thanks, Mickey," Abe said, then turning to me, "I ain't cut out to be a desk jockey,"

"Hey. You did your time on the street. You almost paid the big one as well. You earned this," I said, taking a pull of the cold beer.

"Yeah, I know. It's just hard getting used to it is all."

We sat sipping our beers for a moment, then he said, "So anything new going on?"

"You remember Saul Rubinek?"

"The theatrical agent? Same guy from back with that young girl that killed those actors? What was her name?"

"Lucy Adams. And yeah, same guy, well, he sent a client my way, name's Adele Smithson. Owns a dance studio across from George Hisok Park."

"Hmm. How come? You don't know anything about dancing. I seen you try."

"Very funny. Anyway, she came by the office yesterday and hired me to look into some strange happenings at her studio. Looks like someone may be trying to sabotage her upcoming production."

"Sabotage? Something I should look at?"

"Don't think so, or at least I hope not," I said.

"With your luck, I thought I'd ask. You know, get ready."

"Man, you're a real comedian today," I said.

"Sorry. Had one of those days."

"Yeah, well, as I was sayin'. Her studio has been picked by one of the bright new stars of the dance world to debut his new production. It's been in rehearsal for the last few weeks. About two weeks ago she noticed that things started to happen around the studio, like props falling, equipment coming apart, that sort of thing. Initially, she chalked it up to a series of little accidents. Then last week, her lead dancer, a girl brought in from Montreal, discovered someone tampered with her dance shoes."

"Tampered? How?" Abe asked, signaling Mickey for another round.

"Someone inserted small needles or pins into the toe of the shoes."

"Ouch. I bet that would've hurt." I nodded.

"Yeah. According to Smithson, worse than that, it could've been career ending."

"So, what're you thinking?"

"My guess would be a rival studio. Apparently, there's big money in debuting a major production both for the artists and the studio. It's also possible that it's a disgruntled individual."

"Hmm, sounds like a fair guess," he said, as Mickey arrived with two more beers. "So, what's your plan?"

"Nose around. You know, stir the pot see what rises to the top."

"Funny how they never included that method in the police detective manual. It seems to work so well for you."

"There ya go," I said, toasting him. "Actually, I gonna down to see Gabe at the Riverboat. I figure if anybody knows the skinny on the dance scene in the Village it'd be him."

"Probably right. Hey, listen, thanks for the invite on the weekend. Millie and I had a great time."

"Our pleasure. We gotta do it again sometime."

"Count on it."

We sat around for another fifteen minutes then I paid the tab. He headed home, and I headed for Village. I called Jane before leaving to tell her I'd be late getting home and not to wait dinner for me. I told her I was going to have a talk with Gabe at the Riverboat and would have a bite there.

* * *

I arrived at the club around five o'clock, it wasn't busy yet. There were only a few of the end of day crowd who usually stopped in for a quick drink. I noticed my usual booth was empty and made my way across the room, saying hello to several people I knew. The booth was located beside the swinging door to the kitchen and to the left of the raised stage area. I could hear the dim sounds from the kitchen as they prepped for later.

A moment after I eased into the booth, a young perky, pony tailed girl bounced over with a menu card in hand. Her name was Kathy.

"Hi, Murph," she said. "Alone tonight, or are you waiting?"

"Alone, afraid. Whaddya got on tonight?"

"Pastrami on rye with steamed sauerkraut, Kosher pickle and hot mustard."

"Sold. And a beer, then coffee after. Thanks."

"Okay. Be about ten minutes," she said, as she wrote the order down on her pad.

"By the way, is Gabe around? I didn't see him when I came in."

"Yeah. He's in back. Want me to get him?"

"No, that's okay. Just let him know I'm here and when he's got a minute I'd like to talk to him, okay?"

"Sure thing." She turned and went through the swinging door.

Five minutes later Gabe Herschon came sauntering out of the kitchen. He is gay and proud of it but without throwing it in your face. The Village had a gay population and lately had been more open about it, although, not without a little controversy. As he said, he was what he was and comfortable being so.

He was a first generation German Jew. His family managed to smuggle him out of Germany to England during the war. They, unfortunately, did not survive, dying in one of the camps. He made his way to Canada and established himself in a new life. We've been friends for a long time.

He was a valuable source of information on anything happening in the Village particularly when it came to anything to do with the arts side, being connected with almost every aspect of it through his various 'liaisons' and the circles that he ran in. The only other person who'd know as much or more was Crazy Pete, though his information was from the darker underbelly of the Village and quite a bit seamier.

"Murph, dear boy," he said, sliding into the booth opposite me. "And how is my favorite straight man these days? Still happily married?"

"I'm doing great and, yeah, still happily married. And you? Finally found someone or still smelling the roses?"

"Cute. Smelling the roses," he said with a chuckle. "I like that. Yes, I am still playing in the garden, so to speak. Kathy said you wanted to speak to me?"

"Yeah. I'm doing a small job for the owner of one of the local dance studios and I need to build some background since I'm not that up on the dance scene."

"Well, you came to the right person. What do you need to know? Or do you just want the Reader's Digest version?"

"The Reader's will do fine, I think. If not, I'll ask."

"Right. Where to begin. I guess it would be safe to say that it represents only a small part of the community, but lately there has been a growing interest. Used to be more traditional, you know, classic ballet, but these days it has been moving more towards

Modern and Representational. You know, less classical movements and more free expression of the body. I do so love watching these young men and the way they use their bodies to express their emotions. But I digress, sorry. Anyway, there are a few new, small troupes performing out of some of the old venues that used to offer only music and poetry readings."

"I see. So traditional dance is fading into the background then?" I asked.

"Oh no. Quite the opposite actually. It still has a strong presence and following. In fact, I heard that there is a major production due to début very soon."

"I know. It's that studio that hired me."

"Really? Do tell."

"Have you heard about any group or person complaining about this studio getting the contract?"

"Strange question," he said. "Has something happened?"

"Not sure. Apparently, there have been a few, ah, odd things happening that has the owner feeling a bit spooked and since she's preoccupied dealing with preparing this big show, she didn't want to have this to worry over."

"Oh my."

"Right now I don't think it's anything. Just checking every angle to see if there's something in the shadows. What can you tell me about the dancers."

"Wonderful people. So full of energy and life. The epitome of the free spirit."

"You think any of them would do anything to, say, sabotage another dancer, or studio?"

"Is this what this is about? You think that..."

"I'm just asking, Gabe," I said.

"Sorry," he said. "But to answer your question, I don't think so, if the ones I know are any indication."

"Hmm," I said.

"So, you are here because you would like me to do what, exactly?"

"What you do best. Keep your eyes and ears open."

"I can do that," he said.

"Hoped you would, thanks." Kathy arrived at that moment with my sandwich and beer.

I finished eating and then paid the bill and headed outside. I stopped in at a couple of the other clubs and had a word with several people I knew. Around seven-fifteen I went outside and hailed a cab and headed for the studio and the files.

Chapter Four

The building appeared to be closed and empty when I arrived at the studio later that night. Several people were milling about the front chatting and laughing, many carrying kit bags of various sizes. I didn't recognize any of them, but knew they were dancers. I had the cab drop me half a block away. Standing in the shadow of a stone stair that went up into an apartment building, I waited for the group to leave.

They finally left about ten minutes later, and I headed across the street to the entrance of the building. It was a five story structure with no elevator. The building owner probably hoped to cash in on the arts scene in the Village like so many others had done.

I let myself in with the key Smithson gave me. I unlocked the studio door and went in. Once inside, I relocked the door and headed for her office.

I sat at her desk, turned the desk lamp on, opened the file drawer and took out the file she had pointed out. It wasn't a very big file, so the reading went quickly. Mostly, it contained what she said, names, addresses, phone numbers, ages, and a brief history of past work. It also indicated the dancers that came over from other studios: in this case, two women and one man.

Olivia DeMarco -

age 22, five years with Madame Zola's Dance, joined 1 month ago

Margo Manson -

age 21, three years, Jules Evers Studio, joined 6 months ago

Mathew Henkle –

age 25, six years, Jules Evers Studio, joined 4 months ago

I made a note to talk to these dancers, although I didn't expect to find anything suspicious with two of them, since they came over to Smithson's studio long before she got this gig. However, the DeMarco girl came after. I needed to ask Smithson if any of these other studios had been considered besides hers.

I spent the next twenty minutes going over the file. Nothing else jumped out that looked like a clue or a lead, so I closed it up and returned it to the cabinet. I looked at my watch and saw that it was getting on for eleven thirty; time to head home.

After making sure everything was as I found it, I turned off the lights and locked the office door. I don't know why, but something inside me said to take a quick walk through the studio before leaving. Call it detective's intuition.

I went to the door leading to the main dance area which was across from the office. I went inside and stood in the center of the room listening. It was lit up from the streetlights that shone in through the uncovered windows. Nothing. After a moment I started to turn when I thought I heard a sound. It was barely audible. I wondered if maybe I'd imagined it, so I hesitated a moment. Then I heard it again. It seemed to come from down the hall where the other classrooms were located.

I moved as quietly as I could over the wooden floor to the door leading into the hall and eased the door open and looked around the corner. The hall was almost completely dark. As my eyes adjusted, I could make out the outline of two doors that opened into the classrooms; beyond that, nothing. It felt a little spooky looking into the darkness. The imagination played tricks in situations like this, especially late at night. I stood there for several minutes listening but didn't hear any more sounds.

I debated whether to go down the hall and check out the rest of the studio or leave. It was just jitters, I told myself, feeling a bit silly, as I closed the door. Just as the door clicked shut...boom. Bright lights flashed behind my eyes in brilliant little explosions. My legs gave out and I dropped to my hands and knees. In the next instant a surge of pain burst in my brain. I fought back the impulse to throw up as my stomach reacted. For an instant, I thought I heard or saw someone running down the hall.

When the ringing in my ears eased up and the lights stopped flashing, I tried to stand up. No way. I couldn't get my legs to listen to me, so I rolled over onto my backside and sat with my back propped against the door gasping for air. It was only after a couple of deep breaths that I started to get control again. Something warm and wet was running down the back of my neck behind my left ear. Reaching up, I touched the open wound and, when I pulled my fingers back, blood coated them. My hand was trembling. I reached inside my jacket and pulled out a handkerchief and pressed it against the broken skin. A moment later everything went black as I slid sideways onto the floor.

When I opened my eyes again, I looked around the room confused. Then the pain rushed back, and I remembered. I sat up and waited for the pain to subside then tried to stand. I managed to get up this time and, after making sure my legs were working again, made my way back to the office. I sat back down behind the desk and flipped on the light. Checking my watch, I saw that it two-twenty in the morning. I'd been out for over two hours. Crap. Whoever hit me did a good job. I looked forward to returning the favor.

I picked up the phone and called home.

"He...hello?" Jane said, in a soft sleepy voice.

"Hey, baby, it's me."

"Um, hi...what time is it?"

"Almost two-thirty. Look baby, sorry to wake you so late but I need you to come get me."

"Uh-huh What's wrong? You okay? Are you hurt?" she asked, now awake.

"It's nothing, honest. Just a bang on the head."

"A bang on the head? Wh...?"

"Look, come and get me and I'll tell you all about it, okay?"

"Okay. Where are you?"

I gave her the address and then hung up to wait. She arrived twenty minutes later.

Once we got back home, she immediately became my nurse. She went into the kitchen and poured a pan of warm water and got a clean towel. While she did that I removed my coat and blood stained shirt.

"Come over here and sit down," she said, indicating one of the kitchen chairs.

She went to work washing away the caked blood gently from my neck and around the gash just above the hairline.

"My God, who did this?"

"Don't know," I said, wincing a little, as she dabbed the area. "But when I find out..."

"Well, thankfully, it doesn't look as bad as all this blood would suggest. I don't think you will need stitches."

"Ouch," I said, as she started to clean the actual abrasion.

"Don't be such a baby. I guess this isn't going to be such a simple case, after all?"

I didn't say anything. What could I say? In my world sometimes simple is just another way of saying shit happens.

After several moments she said, "There. That should take care of that, but in the morning you're going to have one hell of a headache." She had put a gauze bandage on the wound and wrapped my head.

"Thanks," I said, turning toward her and wrapping my arms around her waist.

"I love you," I said.

She smiled down at me, as she held my head against her. "I'll make some coffee," she said, releasing me. "Then we'll talk."

"I'd rather turn in to tell the truth," I said, feeling tired.

"I know dear, but that was a pretty hard blow to your head, and you did pass out for quite a while. I'm worried that you might have a minor concussion. It'd be better if you stayed awake for a while."

"I'm okay," I said, standing up. A sudden rush of dizziness forced me to sit back down. "Okay. You win. I'll stay up."

"We'll stay up." she said, putting the kettle on the burner.

The next day I was in my office going through the mail when the door opened. Maddie was out getting some fresh coffee. My head was wrapped in a white gauze bandage that held a pad against the wound. There was a cup of coffee and a large bottle of aspirin sitting on the desk.

"Whoa. I hope the other guy looks worse," Abe said, stepping inside. He went to my coffee machine and lifted the empty pot, shaking it and looking at me.

"Maddie's gone out to get some more," I said.

He put the pot down and came over and sat down. He had a small bag in his hand. I recognized the name on it: Lou's Bagels.

"So? What gives?" he said, looking at my head.

"Got sapped."

"Obviously. Know who?"

"Not yet, but when I do..."

"Uh-huh."

"Happened late last night." I filled him in on what I was doing when I was attacked.

"So, looks like this is shaping up to be another of your simple jobs about to turn into a train wreck."

"Not necessarily," I snapped, not feeling in the mood for our usual bantering session.

"Right. Anyway, the reason I stopped by was to tell that Crazy Pete was hit sometime last night. He's not dead, but it was close."

"Jesus. What happened?"

Crazy Pete was a strange bird and considered by many locals as a 'character' mostly because of his strange tastes in clothes. Eclectic and flamboyant would be gross understatements. But to those in the know, well, let's just say that to underestimate or laugh him off wouldn't be too smart. He's a thief, a hustler, a walking source of information on everything and everybody to do with the underbelly of the Village. He was also very good with a knife as some had learned firsthand. I've known him a long time and consider him a friend of sorts, even so, I still wouldn't trust him as far as I could throw him.

"Apparently, he was found in an alley down by the waterfront near that bar he hangs out at."

"Ed's," I said.

"Yeah. In fact it was Ed who found him. Anyway, he'd been worked over pretty good; coupla busted ribs, possible punctured lung, maybe some damage to one eye. Anyway, the beat cop called for an ambulance and reported it to the duty desk. They passed it up to Willis in Homicide, thinking it was an attempted homicide. It was only when I heard the morning reports that I realized it was Pete."

"So, where'd they take him?"

"St. Vincent's."

"You're looking into this?"

"Naw. But I did send Gus over to the hospital. He says it looks like he took a helleva beating but it didn't look like a case for us. Let's face it, he's been real lucky to make it this far without pissing off the wrong guy."

"Yeah, I know," I said.

"So, what are you going to do?"

"Huh? Whaddya mean, do? About what?"

"I know you, Murph. Sometimes better than you know yourself. You're going to snoop around and see who did this and why, right?" I sat there silently chewing a bite of the bagel.

"Yeah. Thought so" he said. "You're something else, I'll give you that. I hope he realizes what kind of friend he's got ... like some of the rest of us."

I just smiled.

"Back to that," he said, pointing at my head. "You figure it was the person fucking around with the studio? The one that whacked you?" he asked, changing the subject.

"Seems like, yeah. They must've been in the studio when I arrived and hid in the dark to wait me out. Whoever it was, they were good. I didn't hear a Goddamn thing before the lights went out."

"Well, I guess this means you got yourself a problem to solve. Let me know if there's anything I can do, unofficially if possible. I don't need any more cases to deal with, okay?"

"Okay. No bodies," I said, crossing my fingers under the desk. "Oh, you want to know if I get anything about Pete?"

"Yeah, why not. Say hi to Maddie for me. I gotta get back to the office," he said, standing up.

"No sweat. Thanks for the bagels."

"See ya," he said, then was gone.

I sat thinking about Pete. Abe was right about one thing, it had to happen one day. Pete was a rat of the first order. He knew everyone and most of their dirty little secrets. It was common knowledge he wouldn't hesitate to profit from the information. I think that he'd lasted this long because rumor had it he had a notebook with enough information and evidence to cause some very serious problems for some very bad people squirreled away somewhere safe. I didn't know if it was true, but knowing Pete I wouldn't put it past him.

I planned to swing over to the hospital later, or maybe tomorrow, and see how he was doing. For now, I wanted to head back to the studio and have another chat with Miss Smithson. Holes were starting to appear in the investigation that needed filling before the lights went out again.

Chapter Five

The man and woman sat quietly on the sofa. She was curled up in the corner with her arms folded across her chest staring off into space.

The two looked a lot alike, as a brother and sister often do. He seemed to be the older of the two; in his mid to late twenties. Both had fair complexions and light hair. She had a slim figure and long legs, while he stood about six-three or so, also with a trim shape. Both were very attractive, and they were utterly devoted to each other.

He reached for the open bottle of red wine on the coffee-table and poured some into the two empty glasses sitting next to the bottle.

"I hope you realize that you took a great risk tonight," he said, looking at her carefully with concern on his face and passing her one of the glasses. "You were very lucky."

"I know," she answered softly.

"You know this isn't necessary, right?"

"Yes, it is," she said with a sudden hardness in her voice. "He must be punished."

"I know, but..."

"I don't care. What he did is unforgivable. I will never forget or forgive."

"I know and I understand, but this course of action...it's just too risky. And now they have hired this man."

"I know, Paul, but what am I to do? Leave it alone? Go home?"

"I suppose not. But you have to be more careful from now on. We don't know who this man is, he might be an off-duty policeman that she hired."

They sat quietly for several minutes sipping their wine. He looked at his sister with worry in his eyes while she sat staring into her glass. He saw she had changed over the last eight months ever since the operation that ended her unborn child's life. At times, she didn't even look like the sister he remembered back in Montreal. She was so filled with happiness and joy then, especially when she danced. Her whole life centered on dance. Then she met Pierre St. Jacques, and everything changed.

St. Jacques was handsome, sophisticated, charming. She fell hopelessly under his spell. She gave herself to him completely, first with her energy and dance then with her innocence. When she discovered she was pregnant and confronted him, he informed her that he did not want the child and if she wanted to keep it, he didn't care. But if she did, her career, her dreams were over. In the end, she opted to abort, even though this went against everything she believed, especially her Roman Catholic faith.

Shortly afterwards, St. Jacques ended their affair and was soon involved with another dancer, Monique Levesque. It was at that moment something died inside Julie MacDonald, and she began to plot her revenge on him.

The months that followed saw her deteriorate into depression and despondency. She withdrew into herself, and were it not for her brother Paul, no one could guess what she would do. He even tried to coax her to go to confession and talk to her priest, but her shame and guilt could not let her.

"Do you think that he was very badly hurt when you hit him?"

"I don't think so. I'm not really that strong. He fell, but was still alive when I ran away," she said, holding out her glass for more wine.

Paul reached for the bottle again and topped up both glasses. "Well, that's something, I guess. So, what are you going to do now?"

"I want to hurt Pierre slowly where I know it will cause the most pain; his production, then end it with him," she said.

"Okay. I will help, of course."

"I know. Do you know where to get a gun?"

"A gun? God, are you serious?" he said, shocked.

Julie just looked at her brother and nodded.

"Well?"

"Yes. Maybe. I can try. I'll have to talk to some people I know."

"Thank you, Paul. I know this is hard for you, but I must do this if I am to go on. There must be a life for a life. My murdered unborn child demands it."

Paul sat silently looking at his sister, realizing that this beautiful young woman was a stranger to him, but he still loved her dearly. He would get her whatever she needed to help heal the wound in her heart, her soul.

* * *

The studio was in full swing when I arrived. The main room was busy with over twenty dancers going through some sort of routine. Music was also coming out of one of the smaller classrooms down the hall. The door to Smithson's office was closed but I could hear voices behind it. I decided to go and watch the dancers in the main room while I waited for her to finish her business.

I spotted Monique Levesque near the front of the group close to the mirrored wall. She was dancing with a young man performing a complicated maneuver involving a series of turns ending in a slow lift over his head. At the top of the lift, she arched her back so that she had one foot on the knee of the opposite leg which was bent and anchored on her partner's chest while bending toward the floor. Christ, I thought, if he buckles he'll kill her. But then he bent his arms and slowly guided her down his front moving his body through the motion while turning her over so she ended inches from the floor between his legs. Wow.

Just then I heard the office door open and turned in time to see a man emerge with Adele behind him. When she saw me, she waved me over.

"Ah, Mr. Murphy. Just in time. Please allow me to introduce you to Pierre St. Jacques, the choreographer. Pierre, Mr. Murphy," she said.

He extended his hand which I accepted. His grip was surprisingly firm.

"Pleased to meet you," he said, with an obvious accent. I saw that he was staring at the bandages on my head.

"Likewise," I said. "Oh, the bandages. Stupid really. I was working under a counter and banged my head."

He nodded and smiled. "Ah, I see."

He was a very handsome man with thick wavy black hair that looked like it was professionally styled. He had one of those David Niven pencil thin mustaches above his lip. His eyes were clear blue, the kind of blue that women would lose it over. He stood just over six-foot and had a very trim looking body. He wore a tan camel hair jacket over a white starched shirt open at the neck with a silk ascot loosely tied around his neck, dark brown slacks, and loafers.

"We were just going over a few of the staging details," Smithson said.

"Regrettably, I must excuse myself," he said. "I have another pressing meeting. It was good to meet you. Perhaps we will meet again."

"Funny you should say that," I said.

"Pardon?"

"I was hoping to make an appointment to meet with you sometime in next couple of days."

"I see. And this is pertaining to what?"

I looked at Smithson, she gave a slight nod.

"The upcoming performance."

"Ah, oui, I understand, but of course, I shall make myself available. Please arrange this with Adele, yes?"

"Okay. Thanks."

He turned to her and kissed her on each cheek and said 'adieu', then left.

"Please, come in," Adele said, as she returned to her desk. "Have you found out something?"

"In a manner of speaking," I said.

She gave me a puzzled look.

Over the next ten minutes I gave her a detailed account of last night's visit up to and including the attack. The part about the attack upset her.

"This is getting to be more than just someone trying to interfere with the production, isn't it?"

"Maybe," I said. "It was definitely a case of being in the wrong place at the wrong time. I'd guess that whoever it was, had broken in before I arrived then got scared and they panicked."

"Oh, God. This is terrible. What about my dancers? Are they at risk?"

"I don't think so. But it might be a good idea to start checking the studio more carefully when you close up and make sure everything is locked. Might even be a good idea to consider changing out all the locks and make a list of where all the keys are, you know, who has one, that sort of thing."

"God. Is it really that serious?"

"Probably not, but better to take simple and cheap precautions now, when you can."

"Should I call the police?"

"And report what? There's nothing to tell them and they won't take any action otherwise. Besides, I'm on the job and that should be enough for now."

"You mean the police will only act after something happens."

"Yeah, 'fraid so. That's just the reality of it. They have full plates dealing with caseloads and can only respond if something actually happens."

"I see."

I could see that she wasn't too happy with the current turn of events and the limits on how she could deal with them.

"Look," I said, pulling out my notebook and opening it to the pages where I made the list from the file. "I'd like to go over something I found in the file, if you're up for it."

"Certainly."

"First of all, I noticed that three of your dancers recently joined your company within the last six months."

"Yes, that's correct. Let's see, um, they would be DeMarco, Henkle and Manson. Is that something important?"

"Don't know yet. I'm just looking for any connection to what's been happening. I take it that you've had no indication that any of these three, or any other dancer for that matter, has been unhappy or acting suspicious lately?"

"None. My God, you can't possibly think that any of my dancers would do these things? I mean, why? Why would you think that?"

"Don't get upset. I'm not making any accusations, okay? I'm trying to do what you hired me to do: find out if something is going on or if someone wants to do something against your studio. I have to look at everything if only to eliminate it."

"Yes, yes. I'm sorry. I'm just upset with everything that's going on and now you being attacked in the studio. All this on top of all the other problems trying to put this production on."

"I know. When that happens to me, I head down to a gym and punch the bejesus out of the heavy bag."

"And that works?" she asked, sounding genuinely interested.

"Most of the time," I said, smiling.

"Sounds wonderful, but I don't think that I..."

"Wasn't suggesting it. But you should look for something along that line, you know, something that you can beat on without any worry."

I could see that see was considering what I said. Time to get back to the problem at hand.

"So, about these three dancers, you're confident that they couldn't be behind any of this?"

She thought about it for a moment then said, "Yes, I think so."

"Okay. Next item. Can you think of any other dance company that would resent yours being picked?"

"No. I can't imagine."

"Were you St. Jacques' first choice?"

"What do you mean?"

"Did he consider any other dance company before picking yours?"

"Well, yes, of course. That would have been the usual practice. I believe in this instance, he looked at two others."

"And they were?"

"Zola's and one downtown, called the New Dance Studio."

"When did he start looking for a studio to stage his production?"

"About four months ago, why? Is that important?"

"Just trying to build a time frame," I said.

I asked her how long she'd known these three dancers and if her relationship with them was good or not. She said that she knew of their respective work and performance histories and was happy to have them in her company.

I pointed out that Olivia DeMarco had come from the Zola studio within the last month and that it seemed to coincide with her getting the contract from St. Pierre. I asked if this seemed odd to her.

"Not really. When a major dance production is announced many dancers try to get accepted as part of the ensemble."

"She must be a fairly good dancer, then?"

"Yes, Olivia's been dancing for a while. She has a good resume. I was a little surprised when she asked to come over from Zola's."

"What do you mean?"

"Well, I thought she was one of Zola's leads but apparently I was mistaken. She said she was only a member of his first line corps de ballet dancers. When I asked why she was leaving Zola's she just said she wanted an opportunity to dance for Pierre."

"And was there an opportunity?"

"Oh yes, of course. We, Pierre and I, were auditioning at the time."

"Hmm. Obviously she made the cut."

"Well, as I said, she has an impressive resume and it is a small community, after all."

At this point, I decided I had enough to go on for now. I stood and made ready to leave telling her that there several things I wanted to look into. I told her again not to worry and that I would get back to her very soon. She said she would set up my interview with St. Jacques and call me with the date and time.

We both exited the office, and I stood watching the dancers going through their movements for a moment. Adele stood beside me.

"They are so beautiful to watch, aren't they?" she said, wistfully. "I never grow tired of watching them."

"I never realized how much fitness is required to do this stuff," I said.

"Yes, and all for just a few precious minutes on stage. That, and a natural affinity for the language of the music," she said. "Do you dance at all?"

"I can mange to shuffle around the floor without tripping over my feet or crippling my partner. But nothing anywhere close to that," I said, indicating the dancers.

"I imagine you'd be fine to dance with," she said. "You move with a natural ease."

"Thanks. Probably because of my boxing training."

"I'm curious. If you don't mind my asking, what does dancing mean to you? You know, how does it make you feel?"

"Funny, I've never thought about it. I mean, it's just something people do when they're out at a club or a party. When I dance with my wife, well, I like holding her and all, but..."

"Yes, it does feel good doesn't it. That's part of the magic. When a man and a woman come together with music. It's a symbiotic relationship. The expression of joy, pleasure, sensuality and even a little sexuality, within the cocoon of music."

"Never would've thought of it that way, but now that you say it out loud, yeah, that's what it's like when I dance with her."

"Lucky you," she said with a soft chuckle.

Chapter Six

My last visit to St. Vincent's was over a year ago when Abe was here after being shot. Now here I was again, looking in on someone else I knew that was almost killed. I found out what floor Pete was on and headed for the elevator.

At the duty nurse's station, I was told that Pete was still in the Intensive Care Unit under sedation. He was pretty busted up from the beating he took. Whoever did this had a sadistic streak a mile wide and a mile deep.

"Whoever did this must be crazy," the nurse said, almost reading my mind. "I mean, I've seen people who've been beaten before but this ... the guy must have enjoyed doing it. Are you a relative?"

"No. Just a friend," I said.

"He had very little information on him when they brought him in. Do you know of any relatives we can call, or anyone else, for that matter?"

"Funny, but no, I don't. I've known Pete for over ten years and yet don't really know anything about him, not even his last name."

"That we found; it's Shaw."

"No kidding. Shaw. Look, can you tell me anything at all?" I said.

"I guess it wouldn't hurt." She picked up a clipboard and scanned it.

"He suffered three cracked ribs, two broken with one of them puncturing his right lung. Looks like he'll probably lose partial use of that lung, at the very least. There were also two major blows to his head causing a concussion. The rest of his injuries are bad but not life threatening, mostly severe bruising, and will heal in time. You have to understand, your friend has been punched and kicked repeatedly by at least two, perhaps, three people. The doctor thinks he sustained over fifty blows over his body and face. It's simply awful."

It did sound like a savage beating for sure. I remember Abe telling me about a case he worked a while back involving someone who was almost as badly beaten. According to him the attackers were members of a particular motorcycle gang who, coincidentally, were now in residence at Rochdale College. The drug squad suspected they were running a major drug operation from there. That was also where Abe got shot.

I asked if I could look in on him for a moment, but she said there wasn't any point as he was being kept under to allow the lung time to make adjustments. I thanked her and, after giving her my contact information, asking to be called if he woke up or his condition worsened, then I left.

I was really pissed off. Sure, I knew he was a real low-life on the street and would stiff you in a heartbeat, but over time, he'd helped me out on a number of occasions and he never stiffed me.

I drove over to Ed's Pool Hall. That was Pete's hang out. He ran most of his so-called businesses out of there. Plus, he was a well known pool hustler, and Ed's was where he fleeced his pigeons.

Ed's was like so many other neighborhood taverns: an old wooden topped bar along one wall which took up one quarter of the long narrow room with coolers filled with stubby bottles of beer behind it and, a single draft beer tap on it.

Ten well used tables with four wooden chairs each, filled the floor in front of the bar. A single pool table took up the rest of the space at the back of the room with one large green shaded light hanging over it; a cue rack lined a wall with a single bench under it. A small tabletop attached to the wall in the corner with two stools finished off the decor. That was Pete's 'office'.

There were several people in the bar; regulars most likely, sitting idly nursing their beer and smoking a cigarette. Two men were at the back playing a game of eight ball. Ed was sitting in his usual spot at the end of the bar reading the daily race forms. When Ed saw me come in, he stood up and poured me a coffee from the pot he kept under the bar. That had become our routine.

"Okay. Talk. What happened?" I asked, when I reached the bar.

"Figure'd you'd be by," he said, sliding the mug toward me. "Don't know what to tell ya. He was here last night playing a few racks. 'Round 'bout ten these young fucks come in. Three of 'em. Sez they was lookin' fer Pete. Heard 'bout his rep an' wanted a crack at him. So, he takes 'em on at a C note per. Takes 'em five straight. Candy asses. Anyways, they was pissed, especially dis one fella; a real big mouth, ya know, anyway dat's when dey start ta makin' trouble. Dat's when I step in an' kick their asses to da street."

"Were they locals?"

"Naw. I don't think so. Sounded an' acted like they was from somewhere else."

"How do figure?"

"Way they dressed an' talked, ya know, like money."

"You're sure about that?"

"Pretty sure, yeah. Hell, one of them punks shootin' off 'is mouth 'bout being some kinda hotshot wit a stick on some campus. Did no good 'though. Pete cleaned him out."

"Did he say what campus?"

"Naw, but I think it mighta been one a them private places. They don't look any kid goes to a P.S. I ever saw."

"Then what happened? You said something about kicking them out."

"Yeah. They refused to pay up after the last rack. These were pretty big kids, but Pete started to press the kid that lost. That's when they tried to muscle him. I step in wit Mable an' they ponied up pretty quick. They split cussin' and threatenin' to git even."

Mable was a three foot long oak club that Ed kept under the bar for dealing with any trouble. Anyone who knew of Ed's place had heard about 'Mable' and that Ed wasn't afraid to bust heads if the need arose. I knew a couple of guys whod been kissed by her. I hear you wouldn't want a second one.

"Anyways. 'Bout an hour later Pete splits. I don't see him again 'til I lock up when I find him in an alley a coupla doors down the street. He's been really fucked up. Bad. So, I calls the cops. I figure them ass holes jumped him."

"You tell all this to the cops?" I asked.

"Most of it, yeah."

"What did you leave out?"

Ed just gave me a look that more or less said, 'you're kidding, right?'

"Anything else you remember about these kids?"

"Yeah. Two a them was wearin' them jackets, ya know, part leather, part cloth."

"You mean school jackets?" I asked.

"Yeah. I guess that's what they're called. Anyway, that's what they had on."

"Any markings on them? Numbers? Letters?"

"Yeah, come to think of it. They had two rings or sumthin 'round one arm an' a badge or patch on da front."

"Can you remember what it said or looked like?"

He shook his head, "Naw, man, sorry."

"That's okay. By the way, can you remember what color they were?"

"Red, I think. Ya know what da light is like in 'ere. So, you gonna after them?"

It was my turn to give the 'look'.

"Thought so, here." He reached into his pants pocket and retrieved a key and passed it to me. "Said to give this to you iff'n anythin' happened to him. It's fer 'is place."

He gave me Pete's home address, then I left.

"Thanks," I said, putting the key in my pocket then turned and left.

I headed back to the office to check out a few things and my messages.

Maddie was sitting at her usual spot behind her desk reading one of those glossy pulp magazines. She was addicted to them. When I stopped at the desk she passed me two pieces of paper.

"Reading that crap'll rot your brain," I said as I glanced at the notes.

"Sez who?" she said, giving me an impish smile.

The first one was from Jane checking to see how I was doing. The next was from Adele Smithson to say she made an appointment for me with St. Jacques for three o'clock on Thursday at his hotel. That was two days away which gave me some time to look into a couple things before talking with him.

It would be interesting to find out just how competitive this area of the arts really was and just how far someone would go to get ahead. It never failed to surprise me the lengths people would go when money and notoriety was added to the mix. I'd seen its impact on the theater and in the music industry. Now the world of dance. Funny thing though, it always seemed to be centered on those who didn't actually perform, the investors, backers and the like. The ones who actually did the work of practicing their craft or art seemed to be the only ones struggling to survive, except for the few that made it.

I checked my watch: three-forty-five. I picked up the phone and called Jane on her direct line.

"Special Collections," she said, when she answered.

"Hi baby," I said. "Got your message."

"I was just worried a little. You did take a pretty hard bang on the head, you know."

"Yeah, I know. Just a small dull ache left."

"I guess this means you're okay?"

"Yeah. While I got you on the phone, I need you to check something out for me. See if you can locate any private schools with student jackets that are red or burgundy.

Probably worn by their athletes. I'd be interested in any that are located in, or close, to the city."

"Okay. This doesn't sound like it has to do your case," she said. Jane was a very quick woman.

"It doesn't. You remember Crazy Pete?"

"Uh-huh. He's that very peculiar little man you know, right?"

"Yeah, that's him." I tried to keep most of my professional contacts as far away from Jane as I could, both for her protection and because she really didn't need to know that part of the Village.

"Anyway. Abe dropped by to tell me Pete got mugged last night. Pretty bad. He's in St. Vincent's in the ICU. Abe said there's not much the police can do. Not enough to go on, besides, as far as they're concerned Pete's one of the bad guys and, well, you know. 'And Justice For All', doesn't always apply to everybody.

"So, you're stepping in to right the balance?"

"Not really. He's been a friend, sort of, and helped me on a lot of occasions. I figure I owe him, understand? Besides, all I'm going to do is see if I can find something to point the cops toward."

"Okay, I understand," she said.

I knew she would.

"Look, I'm about to call it a day and I was thinking about taking a very beautiful nurse out for dinner?"

"Nurse? Someone I should know about?" she said, followed by a soft chuckle.

"Oh, I think you know who she is. So, whaddya say?"

"I'd love to."

"Any place in mind?"

"We haven't been to T's in a while," she said.

T's is a club over in Little Italy. It's owned by another one of my so-called 'shady' friends name of Elmore Jackson. It's the only black non-Italian club and eatery on the edge of Little Italy. He and his wife, Thelma, run the club. They offer some of the best southern and Cajun cooking in the city and you can listen to some of the best rhythm and blues music around.

We met shortly after Elmore came to town. We were both in a bar when a couple of men took exception to a black man chatting up a white woman. He tried to avoid trouble and got up and left. I saw the two men follow him outside along with another man. It didn't take a genius to see what was up. I usually keep out other people's business but three on one...

When I got outside they had pressed him into an alley beside the club and trapped him against the wall. Then I saw one of the men had drawn a knife. I made my move. The fight lasted five minutes, at the end of which one of the men was unconscious and the other two were trying desperately to defend themselves. I'm a trained boxer and, I learned, Elmore was a very capable street fighter. The streets of Harlem only spit out survivors.

Since that night we've been friends; a friendship that has only grown over time.

Elmore is, in reality, a small time hood working for a black mob boss named, Leroy Paris, aka, Mojo...don't ask why, I don't know. He and Paris went back a long way coming out of Louisiana in the fifties and landed in Harlem, New York, where they quickly made names for themselves. I suspect that there might have been a couple killings that could be laid at their feet, especially, Mojo's. I know that Elmore probably isn't above taking a life if need be, but he wasn't cut out to be a hitter. He built his name on his methods of 'persuasion' and quickly rose in the ranks as an enforcer.

Then something happened. He never talks about what it was, and I don't ask. The result was him leaving Harlem and coming to Toronto. Since then, he has established himself in the city and its underworld. T's is his only legit business that he opened for his wife. I had long suspected he kept his ties open with Mojo back in the States.

He worked with me on a couple of past cases where I needed someone to open certain doors or to trust with watching my back.

"Sounds great. I'll call and set it up. What time?"

"Let's say seven, is that alright?"

"Seven it is. See you back at home."

I dialed the number for T's.

"T's," said a very sexy sounding voice.

"Is that you, Thelma?" I asked.

"None other, baby. Who dis?"

"I'm wounded. Here I thought I was your favorite bit of white sugar," I said, smiling.

"Now you behave, or I be tellin' that lovely bit of honey o' yours you bein' bad."

"Give you the chance tonight if you can squeeze us in. Say around seven?"

"For her, you bet. Guess there be room for y'all too, seein' you with her an' all," she said, chuckling.

"Thanks. By the way will El be around? I haven't seen him in a bit. Thought maybe we'd catch up."

"Yeah, he'll be here. He here mosta the time these days."

"Oh?"

"Yeah. He finally quit the life and stay home."

"And you're okay with that, I take it?"

"What you think?" Thelma was never too happy about Elmore's connection with Mojo but accepted it. Elmore, for his part, compromised by redefining his role with Mojo's operation. So far, everything seemed to have worked out.

"Then I'm really happy for you, T. And for him to," I said. "See ya at seven."

"Okay, sugar. Bye," she said then hung up.

Well, now there's a big surprise. Elmore Jackson out of the life. I couldn't help but wonder what had happened to make him to walk away. More interesting was the fact that Mojo let him.

If he had really given up his ties to that part of his life then I was glad. Don't get me wrong, I never worried for his safety or his life, he was the toughest, deadliest man I knew. It would be no easy task to kill him, even now he's into his fifties. Besides, whoever took a run at him would have to leave the planet because Mojo would burn down anything to find him.

I sat there for a moment thinking. Elmore deciding to get out of the life made me realize something. The clock was ticking. Age was catching up to us and there were things in our lives now that were too important to risk losing. But with age came experience and both he and I were graduates of that school.

I made one last call before locking up: Gabriel Herschon.

"Gabe. Murph," I said, when I heard his unmistakable voice on the other end.

"Murph. Always nice to hear from you. What's up?"

"You going to be around tomorrow afternoon?"

"Yes, as a matter of fact. Wednesday. Ordering day."

"Great. What's a good time?"

"Let's say threeish, okay?"

"See ya then, thanks." I hung up and then grabbed my hat and locked up.

* * *

The blue and white Chevy was parked halfway down the street from the entrance to the club. A man sat in the shadows on the driver's side looking out the window, watching the entrance. The street was busy with cars and taxis and the sidewalks were alive with people walking; taking in the late night ambiance. Hawkers trying to lure them into the clubs, small groups of young people with long hair milling about the steps leading into a tenement building and so on. He could also hear the sounds of the city mixed with those of muted music coming from a couple of nearby clubs. A typical night in the Bohemia.

Paul Dion sat quietly and patiently, looking at his sister who sat on the passenger side, asking himself why he agreed to help her on her path of revenge and self-destruction.

He knew the answer of course; the terrible price she paid because of him. He understood her obsession; the overwhelming drive to exact her retribution on him. Her dead baby demanded it. She would pay any price, even the loss of her soul.

"Why her? She hasn't done anything. She's not part of what happened," he said to his sister as they drove to the club.

"She's part of his production. The main part," Julie answered, sitting on the other side of the bench seat looking straight ahead.

"But...," Paul tried to argue.

"No. It must be this way."

"It will be dangerous to do this, you know. Too public. Too many people to see you, to maybe intervene," he said.

"I will be careful," she said, leaning over and kissing him softly on the cheek. "Just wait here, okay?"

"Yes. Okay," Paul said, looking at his sister as she exited the car and made her way across the street.

"Please be careful," he whispered out loud.

Julie walked to the entrance of the club and went inside.

It was a popular place with the art community, especially the dancers. The room was dark and heavy with cigarette smoke and the aroma of drinks. The only illumination, a mix of colored lights, coming from the small stage and the bar area. On stage, two singers were playing guitars and singing a ballad.

There was a large crowd already in for the night. All the tables were full of people laughing and talking. As she moved through the room, keeping to the darker areas, she spotted several people she recognized, among them, Monique Levesque.

She found a quiet spot against a wall near the entrance to the women's toilet and sat on one of the few empty stools. A waitress came by and took her order for a glass of white wine. She sat watching the table where Monique and six other people sat. About twenty minutes later, Monique and another girl got up and headed toward the toilet..

Julie slipped quickly off the stool and darted into the bathroom. She entered one of the two empty stalls and waited. A few moments later she heard the door open, and the two women entered laughing. When she heard someone enter the stall next to her, she peeked through the crack to see who was still outside. Monique was studying herself in the mirror.

Julie eased the empty coke bottle from her bag and gripped it tightly in her hand. Opening the stall door, she stepped up behind Natalie and hit her solidly on the back of the head.

Monique groaned and slid to the floor.

Julie bent over her and placed her mouth next to her ear and said, "Go home."

She stood up, quickly left the room, and then went out to the street. When she got back in the car, her brother looked at her for a moment, before he put the car in gear drove away from the curb.

"So?"

"Now I must go back to Montreal for a few days. There's something I need to do, but I'll be back," Julie said, staring straight ahead through the windscreen.

They drove in silence. Julie thinking of her next move on St. Jacques. She wanted to hurt him as much as she could before it was over. There was a risk that she might be caught but she no longer cared. Besides, she thought, how likely was it that they would find her, after all, they still had no idea who she was, or anything about her brother. A smile creased her face.

Chapter Seven

The next day I was back at Smithson's studio in the main dance room. Most of the company was there in various stages of warming up. Some were working with the older man I had seen talking to the pianist on my first visit. Turns out he was a former dancer who helped the younger ones with their movements and interpretations of the music. At the moment, they were working a complicated series of turns and lifts.

I was over in a corner talking with Mathew Henkle, one of the names on my list from the file. He was a handsome young man with slightly effeminate features; high cheekbones, clear complexion, slender, some would say lithe, with an exceptionally well toned musculature build. He stood six-foot-tall and probably tipped the scales at one-forty. He had one hand on the bar, the other raised straight up over his head then, with his feet turned at a ninety degree angle, heels touching, he did a deep squat. The muscles in his calves and thighs bulged, straining against his leotards.

"I guess you're pretty excited about performing in this new production?" I asked, notebook in hand.

"You kiddin'?" he said, as he stood up again. Christ, these people were flexible, I thought, as he eased downward again.

"This could be the dance that sends some of us to the really big companies like the Royal Winnipeg."

"So, this St. Jacques is that good?"

"He's the brightest rising star in dance. It won't be long before he's at the Met. and some of us hope to hitch a ride."

He was referencing the New York Metropolitan Theater.

"Hmm. I understand you've been dancing for a while and that you were with the Jules Evers Studio before coming here. Is Adele's studio that much better?"

"Oh, that wasn't why I moved over."

"Care to share?"

"Sure. It's no secret. Jules was moving his company more to the modern method that is becoming popular these days. I prefer to stay traditional."

"I see," I said. "By the way, did you know St. Jacques before coming here?"

"You mean, professionally or personally?"

"Yes."

"No, to both. Look, I don't mean to sound rude, but I really need to prepare, so-o-o..."

"Right. Gotcha, Sorry and thanks for taking the time. Maybe we can talk again."

I turned and ambled around the room. It was then that I noticed that Monique wasn't here today. When I casually asked around, no one knew why. It was at that moment Adele Smithson arrived and stood in the doorway. She waved me over. I noticed right away that she seemed upset, agitated.

"Everything okay?" I asked, following her down the hall to her office. She went and sat down behind her desk. I closed the door and sat down.

"No. Not really."

"What happened?"

"It's Monique. Someone attacked her last night."

"Attacked her? How? Where?"

"All I know is that she was out with a couple of the other dancers at one of the clubs. She got up to go the toilet and was attacked from behind in the bathroom. Someone was inside waiting for her."

"How is she now?" I asked.

"Fine, I guess. She's back at her apartment with a couple of my dancers, resting."

"Did she tell you anything at all about the attack or attacker?"

"Not much. Whoever it was, it seems, was waiting in one of the stalls. When she was attacked, it was from behind and she didn't get a clear look at the attacker. Oh my God, who would do such a thing? Who?"

"That's for me to find out. And I will. Did you call the police?"

"No. She wasn't injured badly, just shaken up and scared."

"Well, you should report this to the police. They'll have it on record and can be on the look out."

"Okay, if you think it's necessary," Smithson said. "So? What now?"

"Now I drop the pretense and go after this person and convince them it isn't worth continuing to harass you or your people. What is Monique going to do?"

"What do you mean?"

"I mean, is she going to quit? Go back to Montreal? What?"

"No. No, she's going continue, just not today."

"Good for her. Look, Adele, I won't mislead you here. It's clear someone means to stop you from opening this production and they've raised the stakes by going after your main star. You're going to have to take precautions."

"What kind of precautions, for God's sake?" she said with a note of alarm in her voice.

"Nothing that'll cause you any more worries. I'll take care of that side. I know someone I can hire to be here at the studio from open 'til close until I find out who's behind this. Second, either myself or another person will always be with Monique. So don't worry, okay?" I said, as she started to say something. "We'll be discrete. The only question is, will you be able to cover the additional costs?"

"I believe so, yes. Can you give me any idea of what they will be? Something I can take to my backers?"

"Of course." I told her I would work out the costs and have them for by the end of the day.

After making sure she was feeling better, I told her that I was heading back to my office to make the arrangements I indicated, then I would be heading over to see Monique. She gave me the address of the girl's apartment and said she would call ahead to let her know I was coming, and it was okay for her to talk to me. Adele also said she would inform the company of the situation and that there would be some changes for the next few weeks.

I headed back to the office and called Ernie Coles. He was a retired cop who supplemented his pension doing odd jobs such as bodyguard, leg work for lawyers, and insurance companies. He never married, claimed he could never get used to the idea of having a woman around that he'd have to talk to. He's in his early fifties and tough as a bucket of rusty nails. I sometimes worked with him I needed help like 'baby-sitting'. I hired him and one of his buddies he recommended.

They were ex-old school street cops, part of a small, loose group of men with similar backgrounds that hired out as bodyguards, security, and other work. They all had carry permits and weren't afraid to use force if the situation warranted. They weren't overly expensive, and I had a solid relationship with them through my connection with Abe Goldman.

I made my arrangements with Coles and asked him to start right away by heading over to Smithson's studio. We agreed this was a two-man job and he said Jake Furtillo was available. I agreed and told him to send Jake to Monique's place and I'd meet him there. I also told him I would be bringing Maddie in on the surveillance.

Maddie had been with me for three years now and had proven herself to be resourceful and intelligent. She had also made up her mind to get her PI license and asked me to help her achieve that goal. I was happy to help.

Next, I made a quick call to Smithson, letting her in on the arrangements I just made and the cost. She approved. I then gave her a heads up that someone named Ernie Coles was on the way to the studio. He would look for her when he arrived and introduce himself.

I was just about to head out when the phone rang.

"Murphy," I said, picking on the second ring.

"Hi, sweetie," Jane said, her voice sounding like liquid sugar in my ear. Instant shift in mood and tone.

"Hey doll, what's up?"

"Can't a girl just call her fella and say thanks for last night?"

"Which part?"

"Both of them," she said giggling.

God, I thought, she made giggling sound like music. "You're welcome," I said. "Look baby, I gotta..."

"Oh, okay. Quickly then," she said, now sounding all business.

She'd found the information that I asked her to dig up. Seemed there are three schools with similar athletic jackets but only one near by. It was the William Academy located in the Scarborough on Victoria Park Road. It is an exclusive facility attended by the children of some of the city's elite families. Their main focus being academics with assaults as an extra curricular activity.

She said she would bring the details home for me to look over. I thanked her and told her I'd look at it tonight at home then said I loved her and hung up.

Chapter Eight

I drove over to the apartment Monique Levesque shared with two other dancers from Smithson's studio. It was located just off Queen's Park near the end of Charles Street West. The area was a popular location for university students. The neighbourhood was not far from either the Queen's Campus, Rochdale, or the Village.

Jane and I were frequent visitors on weekends. We would stroll the various rows of street vendors selling everything from artworks to bric-a-brac. Music was everywhere and we enjoyed the music offered up by the numerous street musicians.

On good days, you could also find small groups of young and old deep in discussion about the state of the world, or playing chess. And then there were the amazing aromas from the many food stands – hot dogs with yellow mustard and brown sauerkraut, Tacos, French fries with cider vinegar and most anything else to tempt the palette.

The street was busy with people bustling about, students heading to and from the University and a mixed bag of people, some with long hair, lolling around stoops and the odd café; some reading, some talking, others playing guitars. Some things never change, some do.

The apartment was located on the second floor of a five story Victorian about half way down on the right side. I climbed the steps leading into her building. The front door was open; the lock was broken. I went in and was met by a man I recognized.. His name was Jake Furtillo; the man Ernie's told me about. I had met him only once about a year ago at some police function Abe invited us to. We shook hands and as we went upstairs. I laid out what I needed him to do. Mostly, he was to keep an eye on the Levesque girl but discretely from a short distance. I would rotate with him sometimes as well as Maddie. As we neared the door, we heard music being played on the other side. I knocked on the door twice.

"Who is it?" A small female voice said from the other side.

"Matt Murphy. I'm here to see Monique Levesque. Miss Smithson called to say I was coming over," I said, waiting.

I heard the sound of a chain slide and then the turning of a lock. The door opened a crack and a cute little face peeked through the gap.

I pulled out my wallet and opened it to show her my license with my photo on it.

After a quick look at it, she slowly stepped back opening the door. Furtillo and I stepped in. "It's okay. He's with me."

She was a very attractive young woman, around twenty-one. She had dark brown hair cut shoulder length which she wore down. She stood around about five-four or five and had a very slender figure with beautifully shaped hips and legs. She had a great complexion and the bluest eyes I'd seen in a while. I heart stopper.

"Sorry about that, but after what happened..." she said, closing the door.

"Not to worry. You did the right thing. Although, you might want to tell the super, or whoever runs this place, to fix the front door."

"Yeah, I know," she said. "We've been complaining about it for over a month but can't get anyone to do anything. I suppose you want to talk to Monique?"

"Yeah, if she's up for it."

"She's lying down, but I'll see if she's awake. Sit down anywhere you like. I'll be right back."

I saw that she was looking over my shoulder at Jake.

"This is an associate of mine who will be around helping me. He'll be around a lot but at a distance."

I looked around the room. Typical student digs, I thought. Mixed bag of furniture; sofa, a couple of stuffed chairs, small tables with bits and pieces of clutter, ashtrays, and the like. Various items of clothing and shoes were scattered about as well as several glossy magazines, mostly women's and theater publications. A small kitchen area with a chrome table and four chairs was off to the right side. Opposite that were two doors, which I guessed to be the bedrooms. There was a single door facing me I assumed to be the bathroom.

A moment later, Monique came out of one of the bedrooms with the other girl behind her. She wore a T-shirt that came down to her thighs and not much else. Christ, those legs. Wow. Behave yourself, I said to myself.

"Hi," I said, "how're you feeling?"

"I'm okay. Just a bit tired. Didn't sleep too well last night," she said, as she came around and sat on the couch, tucking her feet up under her and pulling the hem of the shirt over her knees. Her roommate sat beside her.

The roommate said, "I'm Margo."

"Margo Manson?"

"Uh-huh. How'd you know my last name?"

"Read it somewhere. I take it you spoke with Miss Smithson about who I am?" I said, looking at Monique.

"Uh-huh," she said. "So, you're a private detective, or something?"

"That's right. Miss Smithson has hired me because she's concerned about certain things that have been happening at the studio lately. Sorry about the subterfuge, but I felt it would be less upsetting to you and the other dancers if I seemed to be something else, understand?" I asked.

"Uh-huh, oui."

"Okay then. About last night, can you tell me what happened?"

"We were out last night doing some of the clubs, you know, having a few drinks with friends and catching some of the entertainment. In the last club, someplace called Micky's, I needed to go the bathroom. When I went inside someone must have been waiting there inside one of the stalls. Then suddenly, something hard hit me on my head, and I fell to the floor."

"Did you see anything about the attacker?"

"No. It happened too fast. She hit me then ran off."

"So, it was a woman that attacked you? You're sure?"

"Yes."

"Why are you sure?"

"The voice. It was a woman's voice."

"What did she say?"

"Just, 'go home'."

"Go home. Nothing else?"

"That's right, just that," she said. "Oh, and she wore lavender perfume, or maybe shampoo." Leave it to a woman to remember something like that, I thought.

"Lavender. Okay. Anything else?"

"I don't think so. I was on the floor trying to catch my breath, you know."

"I know, sorry, but every little bit of information helps and the best time to get it is as close to when the attack happened." She sat there and nodded.

Margo Manson sat quietly next to her with an arm over her shoulders and holding one of her hands on her lap. There was something in the way that she seemed to be looking at Monique and caring for her that caught my eye. The arts community is different. It has its own rules and tastes. It is a place where experimentation is the norm; all forms of experimentation. I could see why Gabe Herschon was so involved in it.

"Were you there as well?" I asked Margo.

"Uh-huh. I was actually in the other stall when it happened. There was myself, and Monique, and Jason and Mark. We're all dancers at Adele's studio."

"I see. Did you recognize any other people there?"

"Of course. It's a one of the bars we all go to on a regular basis and hang out."

"Okay. Did you notice anyone in particular that seemed to be paying more attention to you people or Monique, you know, more than usual?"

"No, not really."

"How about seeing the same person in more than one place at the same time as your group?"

She took several moments to consider her answer, then shook her head, saying, "Maybe. I just don't know for sure. So many of these people are regulars at these places. It's possible that there could've been someone, but I can't pinpoint one in particular. Sorry."

"That's okay. It was a long shot, anyway. By the way, have you been with Smithson's very long?"

"Not really. I moved to her studio several months ago. My last studio was moving more to modern dance, and I really wanted to continue in traditional. Adele's studio is one of last to stay predominantly traditional and also have a good reputation."

"I see. And this is where you and Monique met, I take it."

"Yes," she said, looking at Monique with a smile. "We kind of found each other."

Monique smiled back.

Yep, I thought, definitely a different community.

"Right. If either of you remember anything at all, call me and let me know," I said, as I pulled out a card and passed it to Margo.

"So, what're you going to do now?" I asked Monique, as I stood up.

"You mean, am I going to quit and go home?"

I nodded.

"Absolutely not," she said with a touch of anger in her voice. "I will not be bullied."

"Good for you. But you have to be careful. This isn't Montreal. There are some really bad and crazy people here. I'll be doing my best to catch or stop this person, but you need to make sure you're safe. That means not going places alone after dark and, if possible, have someone with you as much as possible. Understand? This man is Jake Furtillo. He's an ex-cop. I've hired him to keep an eye on you. Don't worry. He won't interfere with your usual routines. He'll be in the background but not too far away. You probably won't even see him, but he'll see you. Okay?"

"Oui. I will do as you say," she said.

"Good. Oh, one more thing, if he comes for you, don't argue, just get up and go with him. Understand?'

"Yes," she nodded.

"Don't worry, Mr. Murphy. I'll be with her," Margo said, as she automatically eased a little closer to Monique.

"Good. We'll leave you to get some more rest now. I'll see you again soon."

Jake and I walked back outside.

"You got a ride?" I asked.

"Parked over there," he said, pointing to an old looking Plymouth parked across the street.

"Okay, you know the drill. Anything happens call me right away or Ernie. If you can't reach either of us use your own judgment. Good luck."

Jake would hang around at one of the cafés where he could keep an eye on her building. I went back to my car then headed for my meeting with Gabe.

The club was mostly empty when I arrived, not that unusual for this time of day. I found Gabe sitting at a table pouring over an open ledger and a small pile of papers.

"Gabe," I said, pulling a chair over and sitting down.

"Murph. Nice to see you. So, what's up? Coffee?" he said, looking up and closing the ledger over the pen he was using.

"No thanks, won't keep you that long. Just wanted to see if you found out anything yet."

"Well," he said, sitting back and crossing his legs. "It seems that this new choreographer has created quite a stir. Several studios were anxious to be chosen to stage his latest production. Apparently, a number of principal dancers also jumped into the fray, if you'll pardon the pun."

"Any of the losers holding a grudge?"

"Near as I can tell, according to the boys I know, there was a lot of disappointment but not to the degree anyone would do anything drastic. That's not to say it isn't possible, after all, these are people with very vulnerable sensibilities. I was also told that one studio was particularly, um, disappointed. Apparently, they were the front runner before losing to the Smithson studio."

"Which one?"

"Zola's."

"Okay. Thanks for this," I said, standing up, putting the chair back.

"Oh. One more item that may interest you. It seems that St. Jacques has a penchant for some of his female dancers. He has a trail of discarded women to his credit and, word has it, some of these women did not go quietly, most notably, his last conquest. The word – pregnant – was used."

"Interesting," I said. "Very interesting. Thanks again."

"Always happy to help." He opened a drawer in the desk and extracted a cigar.

Chapter Nine

We were sitting at the table enjoying a meal of pork chops with asparagus and mushrooms talking over the events of our respective days. Domesticity was becoming more enjoyable than I would've thought. Who knew?

I filled Jane in on what had happened to the Levesque girl and my meeting with Rubinek. She also wanted to know what else I was getting into with regard to Pete. I didn't mind telling her. I learned long ago that my wife is stronger and smarter than she sometimes looks. Besides, I kind of promised her when we married that I wouldn't keep anything from her.

"So, tell me. What's the latest on your friend, Pete?"

"As I told you already, Abe stopped by to thank us again for the weekend and to tell me about Pete. So far, all I know is he was attacked and beaten nearly to death. He's in St. Vincent's and on the critical list. Looks like he might lose a lung."

"Oh dear. Poor man. But what's has that to do with you?"

"Well, Pete's got kind of a bad reputation and, near as I can tell, not many friends, except for a bar owner, and me. Looks like there isn't any family either. Anyway, the police aren't going to do anything about it, since it isn't a homicide, and they're so overworked with case files that they aren't likely to spend any time on a mugging of a known felon."

"It sounds like the person who did this is dangerous?" she said.

"Actually, I don't think it was just one person. And it looks like it might've been some high schoolers or maybe some kids from the University or a private school."

"That's why you wanted the information on the jackets," she said, as she picked up her coffee.

"Uh-huh. All Ed had to go on was that they were young and wore these jackets."

"What are you going to do if you find them?"

"First, make sure I got the right ones then pass everything over to the police and let them deal with it."

Jane sat looking at me for several moments, then leaned over and gave me a kiss on the cheek. "You know, you're a good man, don't you?"

"What brought that on?"

"Oh, nothing," she said, smiling.

There are times when I think she is peeking into parts of me that I haven't even looked at, and then lets me know that it's okay.

"So, what's next with the Smithson case?"

"I have a meeting tomorrow afternoon with St. Jacques. I'm hoping to get some idea of what went on during his selection process for the studio. Hopefully, he'll drop something that looks like a clue."

Jane shook her head and said, "It always amazes me how you operate. You go in blind with no clear idea and come out with something that sends you nearer to a solution. I just don't understand how that works."

"It's a gift," I said, smiling.

"Must be, I guess. Whatever it is, you certainly have more than your share of luck, or fortune, or something," she said.

"Not just in my work," I said, leaning over and kissing her.

We were sitting snuggled on the sofa watching the Dick Van Dyke show enjoying a glass of wine, finishing off the bottle from dinner when the phone rang.

"Murphy," I said into the mouthpiece.

"It's me," Abe said, on the other end.

"Hey. What's up?"

"Just got a call from Gus. It's Pete. He's dead."

"When?"

"They called it at seven-forty-five. They figure his heart just quit."

"So, what now?"

"Now it's another murder case. Question is, what're you going to do?"

"Find the bastards," I said.

"Yeah, and then what?"

"Nail their asses to the wall. Then they're all yours."

"Thought you'd say that. I'll help where and as I can. Keep in touch. Say hi to Jane for me."

"Yeah. Bye," I said, then hung up.

I went back to the sofa and sat down.

"Who was that?"

"Abe. Pete died. Heart just quit."

"Oh no. I'm sorry."

"I guess the beating was more severe than they thought. Anyway, Abe called to tell me the news and that it's now being treated as a homicide."

"Is that what you meant when you said you were going to find them and nail their asses to a wall then, turn them in?"

"Yeah. I feel like I owe the guy, you know. He was one of only two people I could go to when I needed information and he always came through, even if it cost me. I'm going to miss him."

"What's going to happen to him now?"

"Don't know. I guess the hospital will turn the body over to the city after the autopsy and he'll be buried by them."

"That's so...so sad," Jane said, looking like she was about to cry. I put my arm around her shoulders and held her close. She had such a generous and caring heart.

"Don't worry. I'll look into what's being done tomorrow. Maybe I can do something," I whispered.

I arrived at the office around ten. My first call was to Smithson's studio. When I was put through to Adele, I asked if my man had arrived, and she said he had and was on the job. I told her I would drop by later after my meeting with St. Jacques. She agreed she would stay at the studio and wait for me.

I filled Maddie in on everything to date, including the news about Crazy Pete which, surprisingly, seemed to really upset her. I asked her to contact the hospital when she was ready and ask into what they were planning to do with Pete's remains. After that, I told her to call Rubinek and see if he could get more background information on St. Jacques, ask if he could give me a contact in Montreal I could contact who might be able to shed some light on the situation.

Around eleven o'clock, I told her I was heading out Ed's to pass on the news about Pete.

When I arrived, Ed was behind the bar setting up for the day's business. No one else was in the room.

"Hey, Murph," he said, as I sat on one of the stools. He came over with my usual cup of coffee and set it on the bar. "Kinda early for you ain't it?"

"Look Ed, there's no easy way to do this, so I'll just say it. Pete's gone."

"Whatcha mean, gone?" he said.

"He died last night at the hospital," I said, filling him in on the little I knew.

"Those muthafuckers," he said, his voice thick with anger and choking back a sob.

"I'm going to find them," I said.

"Whatever you needs you just tell me, got it? He weren't much an' I know that no one took to him, but he was my friend, ya know?"

"Yeah. He was a friend of mine too," I said, picking up the mug.

"Yeah, I know. He always said that if anythin' happened to him to call you. That's when he gave me that key I handed over to you yesterday." That surprised me.

"I didn't know that, thanks for telling me. Look, can you put the word out on the street to keep an eye or ear open. I got an idea that these guys might be running a hustle in the pool halls around the area. It's possible from what you told me that the kid with the stick may have a big ego and, maybe, a bigger mouth."

"Yeah, sure. I got a cuppla guys that run the halls. No problem. What you want me to do if I get anythin'?"

"Call me, or Maddie," I said, as I pulled out my notebook and scribbled a couple of phone numbers.

"Okay. Thanks for the coffee. I'll be in touch," I said. I left Ed's and went back to my car. It was time to go to Pete's flop. I was one of only a few people that knew where he lived. Ed was another, which explained his having a key.

Pete lived in a two room apartment on the third floor of a rundown looking building. It was located down by the docks in the Meat Packing District on St. Clair Avenue near Weston Road. This is a rough area with dock workers, haulers, and laborers. There are several bars and plenty of low end hookers plying their trade to the crews from the visiting ships, and the locals, come payday. This was Pete's world.

After I found a place to park, I got out and went inside and up the stairs to his apartment. I let myself in with the key, locking the door behind me. There were two rooms: the main room which was made up of a combination kitchen and living area. The furnishings consisted of a chrome table with two chairs, a ratty looking sofa with a blanket thrown over it, a small black and white television and clothes scattered about. I crossed to the other door and looked inside. It was a small bedroom with a toilet in the corner behind another door. A single unmade bed sat against the wall under the only window in the room. There was also a floor to ceiling cabinet that contained his clothes.

Forty-five minutes later, I had found several shoe boxes filled with papers and two envelopes. I took everything back into the kitchen area and placed them on the table then sat and went through it all.

The very first thing I picked up was an envelope addressed to Peter Shaw.

It contained a letter from some law firm downtown letting him know that his Last Will and Testament was completed and ready for pick up as instructed. Another envelope contained fifty-three-hundred-and-sixty-two-dollars in cash. Mostly twenties and hundreds. I guess he didn't believe in banks. The other contained several documents: a copy of a marriage license, a birth certificate, turns out he was sixty-three years old; an engineering degree from some college in the mid-west with his name on it.

There was more to Crazy Peter Shaw than anyone ever knew or even suspected.

The last item was a small envelope with three photographs; one with a much younger looking him with a wife and two little girls, the other two were of the girls; one in each. On the back of the family photo, he had written an address: 251 Broad Street, Duluth, Minnesota. There was one last item inside, a small bundle of folded paper tied with a blue ribbon. When I opened it. I held his Last Will and Testament along with IBM and Bell stock certificates. They had to be worth over ten thousand dollars at today's market values.

Two very surprising items leapt out at me. First, he had named me as his Executor and, second, I was to divide any cash between Ed and myself. There was a third item concerning me. He wanted me to contact his wife and give the shares to her for his daughters. Christ, this was a ton of information to take in. I'd need a day or two to let it all settle in and I would definitely have to pay a visit to the lawyer who made up the will.

I made a quick look through the boxes. The only other item of interest was a small notebook. I flipped through this and saw that he had kept detailed notes on a variety of things that were definitely outside the law. He included dates and names. This was definitely going to Abe. The rest proved to be mostly personal papers, such as letters and so on. A quick look through these told me a brief story of Pete's life, from his early days as a family man and an engineer to a nervous breakdown that had him institutionalized for a while, then the eventual breakup of his marriage.

Holy shit, I thought, no one, absolutely no one, would've imagined any of this about Pete, I could only sit there looking at the table in disbelief.

I packed everything up in an old suitcase I found then left, locking the door. I put the suitcase in the trunk of my car then drove back to the office.

I called Abe's direct number and made arrangements to meet him at his office. I wanted to pass Pete's journal over to him and bring him up to date on everything so far.

"Jesus, Murph, do you realize what's in here?" he said, flipping through the pages.

"Not really. I just gave it a cursory look when I found it. Besides, I got a feeling that there are things in there I don't want to know."

"You got that right. Christ, Homicide can solve at least three open murder files based on this stuff."

"Kinda figured you'd find a use for it, that's why I brought it over."

"Thanks. I mean that. I knew Pete was into some shit, but this..."

"There's a lot about him nobody knew," I said, thinking back to some of the things I discovered most of which I shared with Abe.

"Who would've figured," he said when I finished. "Guess it's true; you can't judge a person by their appearance."

I said, "Think it'll change us?"

"Probably not. We know too many bad people."

"Amen."

I got up and said goodbye then headed for my meeting with St. Jacques at three.

Chapter Ten

Jane and I spent an hour or so sifting through everything. Most of the papers were letters written many years ago, obviously between Pete and his wife. The last was a letter from her thanking him for not contesting her application for a divorce.

I looked at the three photographs several times as we read the letters, trying to reconcile the man I knew with the young man in the photograph surrounded by a loving family. We sat a moment looking at the family photos. He looked to be about mid-thirties, she younger. The kids looked about between five and eight. If Pete was sixty-three today that would make his kids in their thirties or early forties today. I wondered if any of them were still alive. Would they have any memories of him.

"I feel like an interloper spying into his life," Jane said, as she finished the last letter.

"Yeah, me to," I said. "I still can't connect all this to the man I knew."

"It's as though he was two completely different people; like he stepped outside of himself and became this total other person even down to changing his persona and set of values. I've never known of anyone like that before."

"Yeah. When I look at him in this picture, I can't see this man as a hustler or a petty criminal. The Pete I knew was these things and worse."

"I guess we never really know the life of another person before they come into our lives. What are you going to do now? You are kind of obligated."

"Yeah, sorta looks that way doesn't it. Tomorrow, I'll call the lawyer who drew up the will and see if I can meet with him. Then, I guess I'll try and find his ex-wife and contact her to make arrangements to pass over the documents."

"I can help with that if you'd like. We have an extensive network of contacts between most of the universities in North America and we're now connected across the country with a large number of major public libraries."

"That'd be great, thanks, baby," I said, giving her a kiss on the cheek.

"If I find anything, do you want me to call you or wait and bring it home?"

"Try me at the office first. If I'm not in, bring it home."

"By the way, what are you going to do with the money?"

"I think I'll hang on to it for a while. At least until I find out if there were any plans made for him from his past life. You know, a family plot with a space already paid for and stuff like that. If there isn't, then I'll use the money to cover a proper burial for him. If there's any left over, I'll give it all to his friend Ed."

Jane smiled, leaned over, and gave me a long loving kiss on the lips. When she sat back down, she said, "Like I've always said, you're a good man."

"I love you to," I said, smiling.

"Now what?"

"Pack everything up and put it away for now."

"By the way," she asked, as she stood up. "How is your case going? Wasn't today your meeting with the choreographer?"

"St. Jacques? Yeah. It went okay. I think I'm beginning to get a handle on what's happening and maybe why. I might even have an inkling of an idea of who is behind it."

"Uh-huh? And...?"

"Sorry, baby. Not yet. It isn't clear enough yet in my head to talk about."

"Okay. So, what's your next step?"

"I think it's time for a look at this Zola studio."

"Funny, but you'd never think that something like this would ever happen in ballet of all places," she said.

"People are the same no matter what their connections are, ballet, business, church, whatever. Anyone can think they've been slighted or done wrong by, and they respond the same way: angry and looking for revenge or payback."

"You're such a cynic," Jane said, shaking her head. "Surely, there are some good people."

"There's at least two I know. I married one."

She came over and sat on my lap, nuzzling her face into my neck.

"Take me to bed," she whispered into my ear.

I stood, picking her up as I did, and headed for the bedroom while she softly kissed my neck.

The rest can wait until tomorrow.

After dropping Jane off at the library the next morning, I made it my first order of business to contact Pete's lawyer and make an appointment to see him. His name was Mark Wilson. I got lucky and was booked in for later that day at two-thirty. My next call was to Rubinek. He was in and Isobel, who must have been in a good mood, put me through right away.

"Murph. How may I help you today?" Rubinek said when he came on the line.

"Good morning, Saul," I said. "Thanks for taking my call. I'll be quick, what can you tell me about Zola's?"

"Ah. Let's see. It's one of the older studios. Been around more than twenty years. Started by Estelle Zola, Spanish by birth, now retired. Living in Florida or Arizona, I believe, you know, one of those

114

hot places. Studio is still hers. It is run by a former principal dancer from her original company. His name is Lecke Mleski. Goes by Lecky. Son of Polish immigrants. Manages a small but very good company of dancers. He practices primarily in the classical style and method, although he has recently experimented with a couple of modern pieces. Good reviews from what I hear. One of the reasons he was high on St. Jacques list.”

“Okay. That helps. Anything special about this Mleski come to mind?”

“Such as?”

“Does he play well with others?”

“Clever, heh, heh; play well with others. Got to remember that. but, yes, he does, although he does have a thin skin and sometimes can take a slight, real or imagined, rather badly, I hear.”

“Hmm. Interesting. Do you think such might be the case in regard to our current situation?”

“You know, I hadn't considered that, but maybe.”

“Okay. That's it. Thanks,” I said.

“By the way, I heard about the incident with our young Montrealer. Is she okay?”

“Yeah, she's great. I spoke with her yesterday. The girl's got backbone.”

“Oh, I also got a call from that lovely young woman who works for you, Maddie, asking if I could provide background on St. Jacques. Unfortunately, I was not able to help, however, I was able to pass along two names of colleagues in Montreal who, I believe, know our friend. I hope it helps."

"You're a star, Saul," I said.

He beamed. The man was partial to flattery, especially the genuine type.

"One more thing. It seems St. Jacques' last 'histoire d'amour' ended very badly. There was a rumor of a pregnancy and abortion."

"Thanks," I said. "This really helps. Look for another box...soon."

"My pleasure," he said, then hung up.

Everywhere I looked, I found hints and clues that all seemed to point back to Zola's studio as housing the likely prime suspect behind everything that has been happening. Funny thing though, it also was starting to feel a bit too 'easy' like them having the motive. Then there was DeMarco's move over to Smithson, but that on its face looked to be nothing unusual and was maybe just a coincidence that happened to coincide with St. Jacques arrival. And now, Saul's news.

Crap, I thought I heard a hint of a chuckle somewhere in the back of my mind. Uh-oh.

Just then the phone rang.

"Murphy," I said into the mouthpiece.

"Hey, Murph." It was Ed from the pool hall. "Jus' heard from one of my guys, Little Freddie. Sez he thinks he spotted them punks running a hustle over at Benny's place last night."

Benny's was one of dozens of neighborhood taverns with pool tables. I wasn't familiar with this one specifically but knew it would be a lot like Ed's place.

"Where?" I asked.

"Up on Scollard above the Village."

"Okay, thanks. Keep me posted. Let's see if we get a pattern or something." I said, more or less thinking out loud.

"Gotcha," he said, then hung up.

"By the way, Ed. I went through Pete's place. Seems he had a will and he named you as one of his beneficiaries."

"Jeez, no shit?"

"Yeah. I gotta a meeting later with his lawyer and once I clear a few things I'll be by with what he left you, okay?"

"Yeah, sure t'ing. An' thanks, Murph. Hey, you find out what they're gonna do with his, ya know...?"

"Don't worry about that. I'm taking care of it," I said.

"Thanks. He'd 'preciate it. See ya," he said, then hung up.

A moment later the phone rang again. Busy morning.

"Murphy," I said.

"Hey sweetie," Jane greeted me.

"Hey yourself. What's up?" I said with a smile.

"I found that information on Pete's ex."

"That was fast."

"I'm good."

"That you are, that you are," I said in a suggestive tone.

"Behave," she said with a giggle. "Do you want what I found or not?"

"Okay, okay. Shoot."

Jane spieled off a name, address, and phone number which I jotted down on my notepad. She said that the information was valid as of this year. We chatted for a few more minutes then hung up.

I looked at the pad. Gloria Jacobson, must've re-married or it was her maiden name, 155 W Lemon St., Duluth, Minnesota. As luck would have it, I had an old atlas in my desk drawer. I dug it out and looked up Duluth. I lucked out again and found a general street map for the city and surrounding area. It didn't take too long to find her street. It was located in an area called, Duluth Heights. I wondered what kind of suburb it was, middle class, blue collar, etc. I checked my watch, ten after ten. Too early to call. I decided to wait until later for the call. No point in spoiling her day this early.

I hung around the office a while longer clearing up some paperwork Maddie left for me. After an hour I headed out for a bite to eat before going over to Smithson's for a chat with Olivia DeMarco. There was something about the timing of her move from Zola's that was nibbling away at me. It was just too coincidental, and I don't like coincidences. My hard earned experience indicated that they tend to become connections with consequences.

When I arrived at the studio there was an ambulance parked out front with its flashers blinking. A small crowd of gawkers milled around the entrance. I pushed my way through and went inside just as two attendants were wheeling a gurney out of the studio with a young woman strapped down. She was crying and obviously in pain. I saw that her left knee was heavily bandaged.

Adele was standing just inside the door looking very upset with a man standing behind her, his hands on her shoulders. I figured it was Ernie Coles.

"What happened," I asked when I reached them.

"An accident," a man I didn't recognize said. I gave him a questioning look.

"Jack Collins," he said, extending his hand. "Ernie sent me. You must be Murphy?"

"Yeah," I said, accepting his hand. "And just Murph is okay. So. Whaddya mean, an accident?"

"They was practicin' a move an' her partner lost his grip an' she tumbled. Banged up her knee on da floor when she landed."

"Yes, that's correct," Adele said, turning to look at me now that the medics were gone.

"You're certain?" I asked.

"Yes, that's what everyone in the studio said. Even her partner confirmed that he lost his grip for a second," she said, stepping away from Jack. "Just bad luck."

Everything seemed to be settling back into its routine as the dancers went back to their practice. Adele straightened herself up a little and went into her office. I followed and Jack went back to his post, wherever that was.

"You sure you're okay? Want a glass of water or something?"

"No. No. I'm fine, thank you. What brings you here today?"

"I'd like to have chat with Olivia DeMarco if that's okay."

"She's not in today," she said, as she sat down behind her desk.

"Not in? Hm. Any reason why?"

"No. She just didn't come in."

"No call, or anything? Is that usual?"

"Not so much, no, but it's also not something that would raise any concern. Sometimes a dancer just needs a down day. Not uncommon among artistic people. You know, just don't want any people contact."

"So, it wouldn't be a good idea to track her down then."

She smiled. "No, probably not. She should be back tomorrow, if you can wait."

"Yeah. No problem."

"Was it important? To talk to her, I mean."

"Probably not. I just wanted clear something up."

"Something to do with this business?"

"Yeah."

"Can you tell me? Maybe I can help."

"It just that I noticed she moved to your studio from Zola's about the same time that St. Jacques made his choice of your company for his production and that it was very shortly after that that he announced he was using the Levesque girl."

"I don't see...," she started to say.

"That was also about the time that your little 'accidents' started."

"Oh."

"Now this is all circumstantial, but there are just too many coincidences."

"Yes, I see. So, you think the attack on Monique is connected?"

"Be my guess, yeah. And don't forget the attack on me. If it was the same person then they aren't afraid to get physical"

"But why?"

"My guess would be that whoever is doing this saw they weren't getting anywhere fast with their sabotage campaign, so they decided to kick it up a notch. Especially after they saw that you brought me into it."

"Oh my God. Really?" I nodded.

"Does this mean that any of my dancers could get hurt?"

"I won't lie to you, if this person, or persons, is desperate or angry enough, maybe. But try and not worry, okay. That's what you have me here for, to see that doesn't happen."

"What do you suggest I do?"

"Nothing for now. Just keep doing what you'd be doing."

"Alright, if you think so," she said. "Should I contact the police now?"

"Probably wouldn't hurt to have Monique make an official police report."

"Monique?"

"Yeah. The attack on her happened outside the studio and didn't result in any injury so they'll likely treat it as a botched mugging or something like that. But it will be in the system at least."

"I'll see to it as soon as she comes in."

"Right. I guess I'll take off. I think it's time to visit Zola's studio."

"Be careful with Lecke. He has a very thin skin and a short temper."

"So I've been told."

She gave me a funny look.

"Saul," was all I said by way of explanation.

She nodded.

"Anything else I should know?"

"Not much. Despite his sensitivity, he was a brilliant dancer in his prime and has developed into a very good dance teacher."

"Okay. I'll keep you posted on how things are progressing." I stood up and picked up my hat from her desk and left the office.

I thought about the DeMarco girl's absence today was a bit convenient. Maybe too convenient. I definitely wanted to talk to her and ask her why she defected from Zola's at the same time that St. Jacques made his decision on which studio he'd use? And, how come this Mleski character seemed to be taking it lying down? You'd think that he would be having a raging fit, after all, he was passed over for a major contract and he lost one of his dancers. But so far, no one seemed to have noticed any reaction from him at all. Curious.

I spotted the light flashing on the message machine when I entered the office. There were two.

The first one was from the hospital letting me know that Pete's remains were ready for pick up. The second was from Gabe asking me to get in touch with him. Both could wait. I had another call to make first.

I dug out the phone directory and found the number of a funeral parlor and called them. After settling on a price, I made arrangements for them to take charge of the preparations and told them that I would stop in no later than tomorrow morning.

I still had time, so I decided to call Pete's ex.

"Hello," a woman said on the other end.

"Hello," I said. "Is this Gloria Jackson?"

"Yes. Who's calling?" she asked.

"My name is Matt Murphy. I was friend of you ex-husband, Peter Shaw."

"Oh my God."

"I take it I'm speaking to the right woman then?"

"Y... yes. What's this about?"

"I'm sorry to have to be the one to tell you but Pete, uh, Peter is dead."

"Dead? When? How?"

"A couple of days ago. He died from heart failure." I decided that it would serve no purpose to tell her the whole truth. She probably had no idea of the life he opted to live since leaving her.

"I see," she said softly. "I... I don't understand why you are calling me. I haven't seen or even talked to him in over ten years."

"I'm calling you because he left a Will and I'm his Executor. He has left something for his children, and I need to know what you want me to do with it?"

"Oh. Can I ask what it is?"

"Sure." I gave her a complete run down on the stocks and shares.

"Oh my," was all she said when I finished. "I guess you could send them to me, I suppose."

"Okay. I'm meeting with his lawyer later today and I'll get him to make the arrangements. His office might call you, is that okay." I gave her the name of the lawyer.

"Yes. That'd be fine."

"One last thing. Do you know if he has any family out there or if you know of any arrangements he made to cover his death? You know, like a prepaid burial site or anything like that?"

"No. No family. Peter was an orphan. I'm not aware of any arrangements either, sorry."

"So, it'll be okay to have him buried here?"

"I don't see why not," she said.

"Right. Well, thanks for talking to me and once again, I'm sorry to be the one to give you the bad news."

"Thank you."

"Oh, by the way, what would you like me to do with the rest of his stuff? You know, the letters and pictures?"

"I guess you may as well destroy them, I suppose. I don't want them myself."

"Okay," I said. "My condolences and thanks again."

I hung up the phone feeling like shit. I'd seen and known the seamier side of life as well as the levels of sadness and misery people endured, but this time it was just a bit too close; too personal. As I sat there thinking of Pete, I realized I wanted to beat on someone: hard.

Chapter Eleven

I arrived at my meeting with Pete's lawyer at the scheduled time. Luckily, the meeting went quickly enough without any hitches. I gave him all the information on Pete's ex-wife, and he said he would contact her to settle that part of the Will. He also said I was free to dispose of the remainder of the estate as I saw fit as Executor, including the arrangements for Pete's burial. By the time everything was arranged and paid for, there was almost three thousand dollars left. I thanked the lawyer and left for Ed's place to conclude my part in handling Pete's estate by passing the money over. I didn't want to take any of the money. Ed got it all.

I still had time to get to Zola's and see Mleski. I drove over to Zola's Studio.

As I drove, I put Pete's business out of my mind by running through everything I had so far on my case. So far everything led to a central point, Zola's. I reviewed them in my mind:

1. They were the leading contender for the contract and lost it supposedly because of a dispute between Mleski and St. Jacques

over the choice of lead female dancer. Was DeMarco that choice?

2. Smithson's little 'accidents' started very soon after this happened.

3. Someone attacked me in the studio after it was closed. Was Mleski behind it or was something else going on?

4. Attack on Levesque. Connection? Or a coincidence?

Zola's studio was located on the east side of the Village on the western edge of Rosedale. It was up on the third floor of a five story office building. Looking up, I saw that it was ringed by high windows facing the street. I could see bright lights glaring from the ceiling despite it being a bright sunny day, much like those at Smithson's studio, so I knew where to go.

The lobby really told the age of the building. On entering you felt you were walking into one of the old hotel lobbies out of the forties. It had beautiful black bordered marble squares on the floor, wood paneled walls and a small four light chandelier with crystal baubles hanging from the ceiling. A staircase that looked like it was made of highly polished oak, lead to the upper floors.

Even the newel and banisters were buffed to a high shine. This was one of the reasons why I love it here: great little gems like this can be found in unexpected places.

I made my way to the third floor. About halfway between the second and third floors I heard the muffled sound of music. I met three young people, obviously dancers, coming down the stairs laughing and carrying bags over their shoulders.

I opened the door to the studio and entered a reception area. Stepping to the desk, I asked the woman who was behind the counter if Lecke Mleski was available. She looked to be in her forties and was comfortably dressed in an Angora top and slacks.

"Do you have an appointment." she asked, smiling.

"Sorry, no. I didn't realize I needed one," I said, flashing her my best and most charming smile.

Must've worked because, she said, "That's alright. I don't see why I can't squeeze you in."

"Thanks," I said, lowering the heat, after all, I didn't want to get her hopes up.

"Your name?"

"Matt Murphy," I said.

She picked up the phone and keyed in a number.

"Sorry to bother you, sir. There is a Mr. Murphy to see you," she said into the mouthpiece.

"Uh-huh, okay. Right away." She hung up.

"He'll see you in ten minutes. Please take a seat over there."

"Thank you," I said and went and sat down. I flipped through a back issue of the Star Weekly Magazine while I waited.

"He'll see you now," she said about eight minutes later. "Just through that door. His office is at the far end. It's the door with the glass panel."

"Thanks."

There were half dozen or so dancers in the room practicing together in front of the mirror that filled the entire wall. In the corner, I spotted a turntable and two large speakers sitting on a table. It was playing classical music that I vaguely recognized but couldn't quite name. Sounded good.

"Enter," Mleski said from behind the closed door after I rapped on the glass.

The office was small but tastefully decorated with an antique oak desk, a couple of old wooden chairs in front and a gray steel four drawer file cabinet in one corner. There was a large one-way mirror on the wall facing the studio dance area.

Lecke Mleski was bit of a surprise. I was expecting someone around Smithson's age, instead I found a man who was creeping up on sixty. He was about six-foot-tall and comfortably carried about one-hundred-and-eighty or so pounds. The neatly trimmed goatee was as white as his head of thick wavy hair.

"Mr. Murphy," he said, as he stood and extended his hand.

I shook his hand; his grip was firm. "Mr. Mleski. Thanks for taking the time to speak with me."

"Please," he said, gesturing to a chair in front of his desk. "What can I do for you?"

"I'm a private investigator. I've been hired by Adele Smithson to look into a series of odd occurrences that have been happening at her studio."

"I see. And this concerns me how exactly?"

"I not sure that it does, but I want to consider every angle since these things started about the time that Pierre St. Jacques made his decision to award his contract to her."

"And you think that I, or any of my dancers, are..." he started to say, a hint of anger rising in his voice.

"No, no, not at all," I said quickly, trying to keep him calm. "As I said, I'm looking at every possible connection if for no other reason than to eliminate it."

"Go on," he said, coolly.

"I understand that there was a dispute over the choice of lead female dancer that led to St. Jacques' decision to go with Smithson?"

"That's correct."

"May I ask the name of the girl you were proposing?"

"Why?"

"Same reason," I said.

He sat there looking at me. Hard. Then said, "Estelle Thurman."

Whoa, I thought. Not DeMarco.

"Not Olivia DeMarco?"

"Certainly not. Why would you think that? And how do you know Olivia?"

"I met her at Smithson's and learned that she moved to Adele's studio shortly after St. Jacques awarded them the contract. I assumed she wanted to get in on the production," I said.

"She is a good dancer, as are all my dancers, but not lead quality. It is only those who have been born with the fire that allows them to transcend the norm," he said, sounding just a bit pompous.

"Uh-huh," I said. "So, Miss Thurman is still a member of your company?"

"Yes. That is her out there. The raven haired one doing the pirouette," he said, pointing to a tall long legged young woman on the other side of the glass.

I turned in my seat and watched her as she was executing a series of turns on her toe, her arms in front of her.

"Beautiful," I heard myself saying.

"Quite."

I turned back to face him and said, "Have you heard about the recent attack on the girl that St. Jacques had chosen as his lead dancer?"

"You mean the French girl, Levesque?"

I nodded.

"No, I haven't. Is she alright?" he asked, showing mild surprise.

"Yes, she's fine. Just a little shaken up but determined to continue."

"Admirable. Do you think the attack has anything to do with the production?"

"On the face of it, no, but I'm suspicious by nature, so until I find out otherwise, I'm going to assume it is. I take it then, that you're not put out by losing the production contract?"

"Of course, I would've liked to have been selected and my dancers perform this dance of his. However, if what you are asking is to suggest that I would seek revenge or some such absurd action against another studio, the answer is an emphatic NO."

"That's fairly definite," I said.

"Zola's is a well and long established company with impeccable credentials and is highly regarded both here and abroad. I have no reason to stoop so low."

And that was that, I thought. It was a convincing speech.

"Is there anything else you want to know?" he asked, his tone getting decidedly cooler again.

"No, I think that you've been more than candid and helpful, and I appreciate your time," I said, standing up. This time I extended a hand which he accepted.

As I walked down the stairs and headed back to the street, I mulled over what I'd just learned about Estelle Thurman. I would have to rethink my ideas about Olivia DeMarco. Something still wasn't adding up. I definitely needed to talk to her as soon as I could.

The next morning, I awoke feeling good, so good in fact, that something else was waking up. I rolled over and nuzzled Jane's neck, slowly waking her up.

"Oh my," she said softly, her voice still heavy with sleep. She eased her hand down between our hips and gently took hold of me. "Mmmmm."

There's nothing so pleasing as making love upon waking. No preamble. No foreplay. No rush. Twenty-five minutes later we were up and dressed.

"You look beautiful this morning," I said, when she came to the table.

"As opposed any other morning?" she said with laughter in her voice.

"You are beautiful every morning, true, but on those really special mornings when we wake like that, well...," I said.

She just smiled at me then leaned over and gave me a soft kiss on the lips.

"Eat, you delicious man."

We ate, content to just enjoy each other's presence.

"So, what's on for today?" she asked as made ready to head out.

"I got to make the arrangements for Pete's burial. It mostly done already except for setting a date and time for the cemetery."

"Will there be anyone there to see him off?" she asked.

"Don't know. The only one I know who will probably be there besides me, is Ed. Maybe he'll know some others, I don't know."

Jane sat quietly for a moment looking a bit sad. She had a good heart, and I knew she would be feeling sorry that Pete passed without anyone to mourn him.

"Cheer up," I said. "He lived the life he chose on his terms. He wouldn't be bothered by no one showing up."

"I guess," she said. "It's just that...oh well. What about the case? What are going to do now?"

"Mostly, rethink it. Mleski threw a monkey wrench in the works yesterday. Up to now, I've been thinking that the DeMarco girl was behind what's been happening, even the attacks. I thought she was the dancer that Mleski was trying to promote and that, after losing the contract, she moved over to Smithson's where she could sabotage the Levesque girl and take her place."

"But not now?" Jane asked.

"No. Looks like he had a different girl in mind. Seems that the DeMarco girl isn't who I thought she was. And there's this new wrinkle that Saul threw at me about St. Jacques to consider."

"Well, you'll figure it out. You're pretty smart."

"You're biased," I said, laughing.

She leaned across the front seat of the car and kissed me on the cheek and then whispered in my ear, "Definitely."

After I dropped her off at the library, I headed to the office.

The day started out overcast and the air had a decided chill in it. Typical early spring day in Toronto. It least it wasn't raining.

It took most of the morning, but I managed to book Pete's burial time for Saturday at two. I called Ed and gave him the time and location. He said he would be there. I asked if he would pass this along to anyone who would be interested in going.

Around eleven-thirty the phone rang. It was Smithson's.

"Murphy."

"Murph, it's me," Ernie Coles said on the other end.

"What's up?"

"I'm at the French girl's place. I think you better get over here."

"What? Is she...?"

"Naw. She's okay."

"Then what?"

"You gotta see this, man. I ain't never seen shit like this."

"Okay, I'm on my way. You call the cops?"

"Yeah. Gus Ferguson's on the way."

"Right. See you in a bit," I said, then hung up.

Fifteen minutes later I was at the apartment. I spotted the unmarked car parked in front of the building. Inside, Ernie was standing in front of Monique's apartment talking to Detective Gus Ferguson. I looked inside the apartment and saw the girl sitting on the couch, obviously crying. She looked badly shaken and very pale. Margo Manson sat next to her with her arm around her and stroking her hair as she held her head against her shoulder.

"Gus," I said, looking back to the two men.

"Murph," he said, turning a bit to face me. He had his notebook in hand, writing down whatever Ernie was saying. He looked as he always did: tired.

"What happened?" I asked.

Ernie tilted his head for me to follow him. We stepped past Gus, and he pointed to the door. I looked on the front side of the door and saw the remains of a large photograph of Monique. It was obviously a promotional picture taken of her in a dance pose. In the area where her heart was located someone had drawn a knife. Below this they had written, 'This is your last warning. Go home.'

"Jesus," I said to no one in particular.

I looked at Ernie, "Who found it?"

"They both did. They were leaving for the studio and when they closed the door...that," he said, nodding at the door.

"Anyway, I was downstairs waitin' for them to come out. It was my turn. I heard the scream and ran upstairs. The Manson girl was holding the other one just staring at the door. I hustled them back inside and called the cops, then you. I figure it was put there sometime before six, because that's when I got here"

"Okay, thanks Ernie," I said, then went over to where Monique was sitting. Margo was still holding her.

"Hey," I said, as I pulled one of empty chairs and sat down. "How're you doing?"

"How do think she's feeling, for God's sake," Margo said very testily. I could see the concern and anger on her face. She obviously cared.

"Look, I know how you're feeling right now, but I got to ask if either of you heard anything, anything at all?"

Monique was the first to answer. "No. Why would someone do something so horrible? Why?"

"I don't know," I said.

"I thought that was why you had that man with us, to watch out for us," Margo said, still sounding angry.

I had nothing to say to that and, even if I did, she wasn't really interested in hearing it anyway. Not yet.

"Did you go out last night and if you did, what time did you get home?"

"No. We stayed in. I have a very hard piece to practice today and wanted to turn in early." Monique said.

"That's right," Margo said. "We were in bed by ten, I think."

"I have to ask this, so don't take it personally, okay? When you say turned in, do mean together? She nodded, "Uh-huh."

"So, you two are lovers then?"

"Oui," said Monique. Margo just looked at me, daring me to say something.

"That's cool. I'm glad you have someone to care for you."

"Merci." She actually managed a smile.

"Have the police talked to you yet?"

"Yes," Margo said, this time she sounded less angry.

"Okay. Are you staying home today or going to the studio?"

"We are going to the studio," Monique said with a note of defiance in her voice. Ballsy girl.

"Good. I got to go now, but I'll be by the studio later. My man will be with you."

She nodded again.

I spent ten minutes talking to Ernie and Gus then took off to find the DeMarco woman.

* * *

Paul Dion stood at the large table bent over a strip of negatives. Two bright lights lit the area from both corners. His left eye was against a jeweler's loupe that he moved slowly across the film. The table was covered with various strips of film and numerous 8"x10" glossy prints.

Just then the phone on the small desk beside the table rang, breaking in on his concentration.

"Hello," he said with a hint of annoyance when he picked up the receiver.

"It's me. Am I interrupting you?" Julie said into his ear.

"Yes. er, uh, no. It's okay. I was in the darkroom. Where are you?"

"My place. I'm just calling to see if anything is happening."

"No, nothing," he said, sitting down in his chair. He had agreed to keep an eye on St. Jacques and Levesque while she was back home.

"So, she's still there?"

"Oui. I don't think she scares so easily."

"Well, I guess I'll have to do something about that," Julie said.

"God, Jules, I wish you'd forget this before you do something you'll really regret."

"No. Never. I don't care. I have nothing left to lose. He killed all that," she said.

He heard the anger and hate rising in her voice.

"Okay, okay, sis, I wasn't saying..." he started to say.

"So, you are still with me then?"

"Of course. To whatever end."

"I love you, thanks," Julie said, her voice returning to normal.

"So now what?"

"I need you to do something. Take one of the promotional photographs of Levesque I brought with me; the one with the knife drawn in her heart and sneak into her building and put it on her apartment door."

"Okay," he said. "When are you coming back to Toronto?"

"In a couple of days," she said.

"Okay. Let me know, so I can pick you up."

"By the way, have you had any success finding a gun?"

"No, not yet. It's pretty risky to get one without drawing attention, especially from the police."

"But I thought it was easy to get a gun?"

"It is, in the States, not here. I know some people who have contacts with some bikers in Rochdale, I think, who might help. The problem is to get one I would have to deal with people who are likely on the police radar."

"Yes, of course, you're right."

"Don't worry, if you are determined to get a gun then we'll find a way," Paul said, trying to sound confident.

"Uh-huh."

After a pause, Paul asked, "Jules, I have to know. Would you, uh, you know, actually kill him, or her?"

The line went quiet for several moments then, in a soft almost childlike voice, Julie said, "I don't know. I want to hurt him. Make him suffer. Make him pay. Dead is too quick, too easy," she answered.

"Good. Okay. I just needed to know," Paul said.

"I have to go now. I'll call you when I ready to come back. Thanks again for being there, Paul. I don't know how I would ever live if you weren't there. I love you."

"I know. I love you to and I will always be here for you. Always."

She hung up and Paul sat holding the phone in his hand.

He hated Pierre St. Jacques even more than she did. He had killed his beloved sister with his betrayal, turning her into this person he didn't recognize. Once a loving, caring young woman filled with happiness, she was now filled with anger and hate. It was very likely that St. Jacques did not even know what he had done and, even if he did, he wouldn't feel any responsibility, Paul thought, as returned the phone to its cradle.

He sat and quietly wept.

Chapter Twelve

Pierre St. Jacques must be held in some regard because arrangements had been made to provide him with a small apartment. I learned later that it was set up by Smithson's backers behind the theater that was staging his production.

I arrived at two-fifty and rang the buzzer to his apartment.

"Oui? Who is it, please?" His voice sounded tinny through the intercom.

"Matt Murphy. We have a three o'clock appointment," I said, leaning close to the panel. "Adele Smithson set it up."

"Ah, yes, of course. Please come up. I am in apartment four on the second floor." The door clicked open, and I went through and headed up the stairs, noting that the inside looked like it was well kept.

"Mr. Murphy?" Pierre St. Jacques said, standing halfway out the door. He was dressed in a pale yellow vee neck cashmere sweater, a pair of neatly pressed dark tan slacks and loafers, no socks. I expected no less.

"That's me," I said, as I reached him with my hand extended and stepped inside. We moved down a short hall, passing a small washroom on the left, to the living room. He directed me to a chair opposite a sofa that could seat easily three. A coffee table filled with sheets of music and a couple of notebooks occupied the space between us.

"May I offer you something to drink? Wine? Coffee?...Beer?"

"No thanks," I said, ignoring the slight note of condescension when he included a beer. "I hope that we will finish our talk quickly since you look very busy,"

"Ah yes. It is no easy matter to prepare for a dance production. Many pieces. Many people."

"Kinda like a jigsaw puzzle," I said.

"Que? Sorry, what?"

"It's not important. Let's just get to the reason for my visit. First, can you tell me who else you were considering to manage the performance this production before you chose Smithson?"

"There were several at first. But, I quickly reduced this list down to three companies. Let me see, ah yes, there was Zola's and The Contemporary Dance Studio. And, of course, Adele's studio."

"Why hers over the others?"

"Well, Contemporary Dance did not have sufficient number of dancers and they were also leaning too much to the non-classical, so they were out."

"Any hard feelings?"

"Que?"

"Did they show any resentment or anger at being passed over?"

"Ah I understand. No. No hard feelings."

"What about Zola's?"

"A good company. They were a very close second choice, yes."

"And they were rejected because...?"

"A disagreement over selection of lead female dancer. Their dancer was very good, but I have my choice."

"Monique Levesque."

"Oui. A very gifted dancer who instinctively understands the marriage of movement and music. Incredible."

"So, Zola's was probably upset when you passed them over?"

"Yes, a little, I think," St. Jacques said, sitting back and crossing his legs; his movements were very relaxed, fluid.

"Do you know about the things that have been happening at Smithson's studio lately?"

"I have heard something, yes, but I am assured that it is nothing that will affect the production."

"Did you know that Monique was attacked yesterday?"

"Mon dieu, no," he said, sitting up and leaning forward. "Is she...?"

"Yes. She's fine. I spoke with her. She's a little upset but not hurt. She intends to go on with the production."

"Very good, very good. I must call on her."

"Just out of curiosity, do you happen to know the name of the dancer that Zola wanted to use?"

"I do not remember, I'm afraid. Sorry."

"That's okay," I said. I already knew her name. "Well, that's all I need for now. I'll let you get back to your work. Thanks for giving me the time," I said, standing and offering him my hand again which he accepted.

He walked me back to the door and after saying goodbye, I went back down to back to the street. I looked at my watch; three-forty. I headed for Smithson's studio.

Adele Smithson was sitting in her office talking on the phone. I waved to let her know I was there then went to look for Ernie Coles. I spotted him standing off to one side in the main dance studio. I also spotted Monique in the room going through a routine with a young male dancer while an older man with a stick tapped out the time on the floor. The girl has spunk, that's for sure, I thought, as I stepped over to Ernie.

"Everything okay?" I asked in a low voice so as to not disturb the dancers.

"Yeah. Everythin's cool."

"When'd you get here?"

"Early."

"Who's up next?"

"Maddie. Should be along soon."

I sometimes let Maddie in on the odd case I was working on so she could gain some experience. When I hired her on she indicated that she thought she would like to learn the trade and get her own license. I was happy to help. She's smart, quick and has good intuitive instincts. Besides, this was just the type of case where she, as a woman, could prove invaluable.

Just then I saw Adele standing in the door.

"Okay. I'll keep in touch," I said. I stepped over to the door and followed her into her office and closed the door.

"How did your meeting go with Pierre?" she asked, as she sat down.

"Not too bad. He did say that the Zola studio was a serious contender for his production and that the main reason they lost out was a dispute over who the female lead was going to be. Was it really that close?"

"Yes. It was. You have to understand. In our world, having a leading star, established, or recognized as being on the rise, is critical to the success of a studio. Choreographers are always wanting the very best dancers that have the critic's eye to showcase their work and, of course, these dancers want to be chosen to establish their careers."

"Sounds pretty symbiotic," I said, throwing out one of my ten dollar words. Advantage of being hooked up with a librarian.

"Mmm, quite," she said, cocking an eyebrow.

"So, I guess there is a high degree of competition, you know, between studios, dancers."

"Oh yes, but I have never heard of it escalating to the level of violence, especially against another dancer."

"Well, something is going on here. These incidents in your studio may seem coincidental to you, but from what I've seen, if any of these had happened to a dancer I suspect they would've been injured. And I think this attack on Levesque was deliberate and was intended as a warning."

"My God," she said, sitting back. "A warning? To do what?"

"Monique said the attacker told her to leave town, go back to Montreal. I'm guessing that whoever attacked her knows who she is and why she's here, but don't worry, she said wouldn't be intimidated and that she was staying. The girl's got spunk, I'll give her that."

"So, what should I do? I mean, no show is worth risking the life of my dancers."

"My advice would be to continue. I've got a couple of good people working on this with me now, so I think you shouldn't have any more trouble at the studio. As for outside, I've taken care of that part as well. Okay?"

"If you think so, then yes. Thank you. How long do you think this will go on?"

"Don't know, but I'm good at what I do, and I will find out who's behind this and stop them." I hoped that I sounded confident enough to put her mind at ease. Hell, I almost convinced myself. "Now, what can you tell about Zola's?"

I left the studio fifteen minutes later. Smithson had given me a summary background of the Zola's studio as well as the dance, Olivia DeMarco, the ballerina who left them for Adeles studio.

It was time I had a talk with Miss DeMarco.

Olivia DeMarco lived in a small house on Huron Street, three and a half blocks down from Bloor Street W. I parked the car across from the house and got out. I climbed the three steps onto a covered porch, went to the front door, and knocked. Nothing. I knocked again and waited. Again, nothing, so I went back to my car and got in.

I went back to Zola's studio on the off chance I might find someone who DeMarco knew well enough to give me an idea of where she usually spent her time when not dancing.

When I arrived at the studio I went inside and headed for the office. The door was open. Mleski was sitting at his desk and two women dressed in dancing costumes were standing in front of him. He sounded upset.

"Yes? What do you want?" he said, when he spotted me standing at the door.

"Remember me," I said. "Murphy?"

"Yes, yes. What now?"

The two young women scooted past me as I stepped aside.

"I was hoping you could tell me if any of your dancers were friends with DeMarco?

"Of course, there were. She was a likable person. Why?"

"I've been looking for her and, well, I can't seem to find her, not at Smithson's or at her home. I was hoping that one her friends might be able to tell some places she frequents."

"I see," he said, turning to face me. "Speak with Estelle Casey. She's in studio A, two doors down the hall. They were fairly close as I recall."

"Thanks," I said.

I found Estelle in the mirrored room going through a series of movements. She was like most of the other women I've met since starting this case. Tall. Statuesque. Young. Beautiful. I reckoned her to be about twenty-two. She wore her dark brown hair in a page boy cut which accented her long neck and face wonderfully.

"Excuse," I said when I stepped into the room. "My name's Matt Murphy."

"I know who you are," she said. "You're that detective Adele hired."

Interesting. How did she know who I was and what I did?

"That's right. I was hoping we could have a talk if you would spare the time?"

"Certainly," she said. I noted there was an almost musical quality to her voice. "We can speak over there if you like."

She led us to an empty corner of the dance floor.

"Thanks. I won't keep you long."

"That's alright, I could use a bit of a breather. You don't mind if I stretch a bit do you? I don't want my muscles to cool down."

"Not a problem. I have been trying to reach Olivia DeMarco to speak with her, but without any success. I'm hoping you can tell me where I might be able to find her?"

"Have you tried our place?"

"Oh, you two live together?" I asked.

Well, that answered the question about knowing who I was. DeMarco must have heard about me at Smithson's and told her.

"Uh-huh. We have a small set of rooms on Huron Street," she said as she flexed her left leg, raising the knee chest high then, sliding her hand to the ankle, pulled it straight up, arching her foot as she pointed at the ceiling. Christ, but that was so distracting.

"Yes, I've been there. No luck." I hoped I sounded cool and collected as I tried to not stare at the sensuous leg.

"Hm, let me think," she said, slowly lowering her leg. I was sure she was doing this for my benefit. Hey, works for me.

"Oh yes. This is the day she usually goes to the Riverboat. She works there part-time as a waitress. Dancing doesn't pay an awful lot and, like everyone else, we have bills to pay."

"The Riverboat, right. Thanks," I said as I started to walk away. "By the way, if you don't mind my saying, you are one of the most beautiful women I've seen."

"Now why would I mind you, or anyone, saying that?" she said with a very suggestive look. I guess she was one of those sexually liberated women I've read about in one of Maddies' magazines.

Chapter Thirteen

Most of the clubs wouldn't be open for much more than a coffee and sandwich before eight o'clock. I decided to head over there anyway.

When I reached Yorkville Avenue it was packed with people...as usual.

The sidewalks were crammed already with hippies and tourists coming to see the 'wildlife'. Most of the denizens were young; between fourteen and thirty – the younger ones most likely were runaways who hitched a ride here from who knew where.

Everywhere you looked, you saw bell-bottomed jeans, shabby jackets, and long hair, and once in while you could pick up the faint aroma of 'weed'. A few of the shops had music drifting out from open doors.

It was a nice spring day so most of the clubs that had patio service were enjoying a steady trade. I reached the Riverboat and went inside. I spotted a waitress serving a table with a couple sitting at it.

"Excuse me," I said when she finished serving them.

"Yes?" she said. She was obviously part of the new age scene: Long dark brown hair parted in the middle, no make-up, floral patterned long skirt, and sandals. If I had to hazard a guess, I would have to say she was probably an inhabitant of Roshdale.

"I'm looking for Olivia DeMarco. One of her friends she said might be working today."

"Uh-huh, that's her over there." She pointed to the far side of the room where Olivia was standing at a counter.

She was striking to look at even in this dim light; tall and slender. She had short cut black hair that came to an inch above her shoulders. Unlike the first girl, she was dressed in jeans and t-shirt.

They seemed to be everywhere, and I felt embarrassed that, as an experienced PI, I never noticed before.

She turned her head toward me as I approached.

"Miss DeMarco?" I asked.

"Yes," she said, flashing a warm smile with a set of the whitest teeth I seen.

"My name is Matt Murphy," I said. "I've been hired by Adele Smithson to look into the accidents that have been plaguing her studio lately and I have been talking with her dancers."

"You a cop?"

"No. A private detective."

"No shit. Wow. A real P.I."

I couldn't be sure if she was being genuine or yanking my chain.

"Can we go somewhere for a coffee and talk?"

She nodded. "There's a place we go to nearby."

After telling the man she was talking to when I arrived that she was taking a break, she led the way out of the building and took me down the street about a block and a half away to a small deli. It was still fairly quiet inside so we easily found a table in a corner where we could talk. I ordered coffee and sandwiches for both of us. She passed on the sandwich.

"So?" I opened the conversation. "I understand that up to recently, you were dancing at Zola's? I was wondering why the move to Smithson's?"

"Artistic differences," she said as the waiter arrived with our orders.

"Not for a chance to dance for St. Jacques?"

"Well, of course..."

"But not in a leading role I heard."

"No. He already had his lead. It was quite enough to be cast in the production."

I didn't detect any anger or resentment in her answer, in fact, she seemed quite happy about her decision. This was looking more and more like a dead end.

"So, you're happy at Smithson's?"

"Yeah...sort of."

"You don't sound too sure."

"Don't get me wrong. Adele is great and really well liked and respected. It just that since I arrived at the studio things have been happening but, you know that already."

"Good point," I said.

"Anyway, I have been thinking about going back to Zola's after the production wraps up its run here...unless I get an offer to stay on for the tour."

"Does Adele know that, or Mieski, for that matter?" I asked.

"Yes, I discussed it with her, wanting her advice. And I met with Mieski the other day."

Funny Mieski didn't mention this when we talked.

"How'd they take it?'

"Adele was understanding, but he was angry because I was asking if he would take me back into the company."

"And why would you want to return to Zola's?"

"It's a very good company and they put on very good productions, besides, it's one of the few companies around that will still use us older dancers."

Old! She had to be kidding. She had to be not a day over thirty.

"I know what you're thinking. But in dance, age matters." She said, as if reading my mind.

"Was that why you moved over to her studio?"

"Partly. The classical style is more experience based, you see. Besides, it was also a great opportunity for a dancer. It could have led to other dances with some of the best choreographers in the dance world. Maybe even abroad."

"I see. So why was Mleski so upset? I'd a thought he'd be happy to get one of his dancers back?"

"I was never under the illusion that he thought of me as anything more than second string dancer, but he did tell me once that I was one of his best in that role. I think he was angry because when I left for Adele's. He felt that I betrayed him."

"So, is he going to take you back?"

"I think so. Estelle backed me up."

"And why would that make a difference?"

"She's his principal ballerina." She said this as if it was obvious. Right.

"So, what's the connection between you two?" I asked.

"Estelle and me? We live together and are very good friends."

"I see," I said. It must have been something in my tone that she picked up on.

"Oh, not like that. We have a two bedroom apartment. I mean, we have tried it once or twice, but we decided that, even though it was a nice experience, we both prefer men."

"Lucky guys. I wasn't making any assumptions or judgments. You're adults."

"Thank you for that," she said.

"Can you tell me how Estelle felt when St. Jacques chose Adele's studio and the Levesque girl instead of Zola's and her?"

"She was very disappointed, of course. Who wouldn't be. After all, this was great opportunity like I've already said."

"By the way, can you tell me where you both were last night?"

"Why?"

"It's a detective thing. Can you tell me?"

"We were both at home watching T.V. Has something else happened?"

"There was another incident, yeah. No one was hurt," I said. I didn't need to go into details.

"So, you were thinking we were suspects? Or maybe just me?"

"I'm a detective. We think everyone is a suspect until proven otherwise."

"And now?" she challenged.

"Let's say that you're getting farther down the list near the bottom."

"I guess that's something. I should be upset, but I understand."

"Can you think of anyone who would want to sabotage this performance or hurt the Levesque girl?"

"God, no," she said.

"So, you didn't see or hear anything unusual or out of place while you were at Smithson's?"

"Not really. I mean, I wasn't aware of anything, why would I have been."

"Did you know all the dancers in her company?"

"Yes, most of them. It's a small community and we have danced together at different times."

"So, no one new or anyone you didn't know?"

"Of course, there are always new faces but, in this case, I knew most or recognized them."

I signaled the waitress to bring the bill. I asked if she wanted me to walk her back to the studio or give her a lift home. She declined, saying she would stay here and have another coffee while she waited for Estelle. This was their usual lunch spot.

"Okay then. I'm about done here. Thanks for talking to me and being so frank. I appreciate it. Good luck with Mleski."

"Oh, that's going to be okay. Thanks anyway and thanks for this," she said, lifting her cup.

"My pleasure."

I was about to get up when she said, "Just a sec."

"Yes?" I said, settling back on the chair.

"I just remembered something. It was shortly before I left Zola's and we heard that St. Jacques was coming to Toronto to stage his production."

"Go on."

"Word is that he has a reputation of having affairs with his dancers and that most have not ended well."

"That it?" She nodded.

"Apparently, his last liaison was with a dancer who became pregnant and had to leave his company. Some heard that he actually dismissed her. Mind you, this is all rumour, of course and we are notoriously 'catty' when it comes to anything salacious."

I thanked her again. I stood up and left her there. Back on the street, I made my way back to my car and went back to the office.

As I drove, I considered this new angle she put forward. So far, every thread I found and pulled came up with zilch. My two prime candidates were now a bust. Mleski wasn't overly put out over losing to Smithson's studio which, on the face of it seemed odd, but having met him, I was inclined to believe him. Then there was DeMarco. I was satisfied that she wasn't behind this business since she had nothing to gain. All of this left me where I often end up: nowhere. Now I had a new lead: St. Jacques and Montreal and this pregnant dancer.

I wasn't in the office for thirty minutes when Abe showed up carrying a bag of bagels. He really must not like desk work; he didn't visit me this much when he worked the street. Not that I minded, after all, he is my best friend, and he always brings good bagels.

"Beware cops bearing bagels," I said, as he closed the door then tossed me the bag.

"Cute. Thought I'd stop by and see if you heard anything about those people that did Pete," he said, stepping over to the coffee machine. He poured himself a cup and then held the pot toward me.

I nodded.

He came over and sat on one of the two chairs in front of my desk. I opened the bag and discovered two fresh baked bagels inside. I tore the bag down the side and took one then pushed the other across to Abe.

"I'm working on it.," I said, taking a bite.

"Meaning?"

"Meaning, I got some feelers out. I can say that it's beginning to look like it was two or three high school students or maybe juniors from one of the colleges. Don't know which yet." Abe nodded.

"So, you're still runnin' with this avenue of inquiry based on Ed saying' one of them was wearin' what you believe was a school jacket?" I nodded.

"Anyway, Ed's put the word out with some of his contacts to keep an eye open."

"Why you figuring that'll do any good?"

"I'm playing a hunch."

"Want to share? I mean, I'm just a lowly cop and this might be a learning experience."

"Good thing you know a good bakery," I said, finishing off the bagel.

He chuckled as he picked up his mug.

"This thing started with these punks trying to hustle Pete on the table. According to Ed, Pete took them for a couple of hundred and they tried to stiff him. Anyway, Pete and Ed braced them, they paid up and then split. According to Ed, the kid with the stick was mouthing off about how good he was and figured he was running the halls in the area, trying to make a name for himself. Seems the kid had a real ego issue. I'm figuring, if it's as big an ego as it sounds, then he won't stay away for long and will try to run his hustle again. If he does, and one of Ed's guys spots them, and gets it back to me then..."

"Then you'll pay them a visit, I know," he said finishing my statement.

I smiled.

"You know that we don't have a single piece of hard evidence that these kids did it, right?"

"Yeah, but I'm satisfied."

"That ain't enough. You're basing everything on questionable secondhand information and even if it weren't dubious, it would still be circumstantial at best."

"I know. But I'm counting on one thing to cinch it. The kid with the ego. There's something he doesn't know, and you obviously haven't tweaked onto yet," I said sitting back.

"Please. Enlighten me," he said sarcastically.

"Pete's wallet."

"Pete's wallet? What the hell are you talking about?"

"After he died, I went to the hospital to collect his clothes and noticed his wallet was missing. I made some inquiries and gathered that no one had been in his room. The I.C.U. is tightly monitored.”

“Yeah, okay, so what about the wallet?”

“Pete had a very distinctive wallet. I saw it several times and even asked about it. He'd only say that he got it from some pigeon he plucked in a game a long time ago. The wallet was made from real snakeskin and had turquoise inlays in the corners.”

“And you're thinking this kid took it.”

“That'd be my guess, yeah. I'm thinking he's cocky enough to think of it as a trophy.”

“Hmm, not bad. Not bad at all. If you find this kid and he has the wallet then what?”

“Wrap him in a bow and deliver him to Gus.”

“Works for me. Okay. I better get back. The paperwork won't go away until I do. Oh, by the way, how're you doing with his Will?”

“I spoke to the lawyer and the ex-wife and everything is settled. I made the funeral arrangements for Saturday.”

I gave him the name of the cemetery and the time. I told him Jane and I would be there to see him off. I knew he wouldn't show up. It was a good guy, bad guy thing.

“Thanks, by the way,” I said, holding up the torn bag and shaking it.

“No problem. Your treat next time. Say hi to Jane for me. See ya,” he said then left.

Okay. Now back to the business at hand.

I couldn't think of any place to go. My main leads had proved to be dead ends. But now there was this new wrinkle that DeMarco laid on me which seemed to jibe with Saul's information.

And, someone was still out there waiting to do more mischief, or worse.

I thought back over the last few days following the threads and connecting the dots, trying to find something, anything, I might've missed. Initially, it looked like someone was out to sabotage Smithson's studio but then it turned against Monique Levesque.

It started with a series of mishaps; the falling props and loose equipment then escalated to more sinister things like the girl's shoes and the pins. It'd be interesting to find out if she was in any of the areas when the so-called accidents happened. Perhaps the so-called accidents were staged as a diversion to direct attention away from the main purpose, take out Levesque. But if that was the case, then who was behind it? And why?

I could only think of three options where the answer might lie: It was someone from within the local community who lost this opportunity and wanted revenge, or it was something specific to the girl, or maybe it has something to do with St. Jacques.

Maybe I've been looking at this all wrong. Maybe the things that were happening followed her here from Montreal? I needed to talk to Smithson and the girl again. I needed to take a closer look at Pierre St. Jacques.

The way things were shaping up, it looked like a trip to Montreal was staring at me.

Chapter Fourteen

I got to Levesque's apartment around four. I knocked on the door and waited.

"Who is it?" a voice said from behind the door.

"Matt Murphy," I answered.

I heard a chain slide then a lock turn. It was Margo Manson who opened the door. She was wearing a long t-shirt and a pair of shorts and not much else. I had to say she made it look good.

As I stepped inside, I was met with a pleasant aroma of something being cooked.

"Mmm, smells good," I said.

"Thanks," she said as she closed the door and she gestured for me to sit down in the small living room. "Monique's a wonderful cook."

She followed me into the room and sat down on the sofa, tucking her bare legs under her.

"Can I offer you something to drink? We've got wine and I think there's still some beer in the fridge."

"No thanks, I'm good. How're you two doing now?" I asked her.

"Much better, thanks," she said. "So? Do you have any idea who's doing these things yet?"

I heard a door open behind me and Monique came in carrying a glass of wine. She went and sat beside Margo. They both looked at me, waiting for me to say something.

"I'm getting closer."

I looked at Monique and said, "Actually, I stopped by to talk with you about Montreal."

"Montreal? I don't understand," Monique said, setting her glass down on the coffee table.

"Tell me about how you and St. Jacques met and the studio where you danced," I said.

"Pierre? I met him during a exhibition performance the company I was with put on at a local community center."

"When was that?"

"About three months ago, I think."

"Was that the first time you met him or heard of him?"

"Met him yes, although, I heard about him before like all professional dancers. He is very well known in Montreal, even in New York, I hear. I also heard he was once a student of my studio's owner, Monsieur Gaudet. Although, since then, he has staged several very successful productions with very good reviews. He is a brilliant choreographer."

"Did he come to the performance to meet you specifically?"

"No. I think Monsieur Gaudet invited him to attend. I learned later that he was scouting for dancers for his newest production and was doing informal auditions by going to various studios and exhibitions," she said.

"Why all these questions about Pierre?" Margo asked.

"Just part of the process, you know, getting as much background on anyone connected to the case that's all," I said.

"Surely you do not suspect Pierre?" Monique asked, sounding a little startled.

"No. No, of course not. I'm just looking for information that'll hopefully lead me to finding the person behind these things that have been going on. When you moved to St. Jacques' company did you ever have any contact with him outside of dancing?"

"Que? Outside?" Monique said with a slightly puzzled look on her face.

"Yeah, you know, on a personal level."

"Oh, I understand. You mean did we sleep together? No. Oh, he did try to initiate something at the beginning but, as you see, I have, um, different, how you say, preferences."

"And he didn't mind?"

"No, not that I ever noticed. Besides, I think he is never in want of someone to warm his bed," she said with a sly smile.

"So, you must be very good...at dancing."

She gave me another funny look.

"Usually when a man's advances are rebuffed they don't re-act well." I said.

"Oh, I see. He does not let that, or anything, come between him and his dance."

"Speaking of his, um, 'activities', did you happen to hear any rumours or stories about that side of his reputation?"

"Pardon?"

"You know, like bad feelings after he moves on to someone else, that sort of thing?"

"There are always rumours, stories, circulating in a community like ours," Margo stated, joining the discussion. "As you probably guessed by now, most of the dancers have somewhat more liberal sexual values. We are a very sensitive and very much in touch with that part of our nature."

"Uh-huh. Do you know who they were?"

"His paramours? No. Sorry."

"But there are exceptions I take it?"

"Like most things in life, yes. Some dancers are even married with families, though not that many. Dancing takes everything from us, physically and emotionally. Usually there is not much left to give to a relationship, especially a heterosexual one. It is easier and more rewarding to be with someone who understands."

Monique reached a hand over and covered one of Margo's hands.

"I get that," I said.

I was rewarded with two beautiful smiles.

"Did you ever hear of any relationship between St. Jacques and his female dancers that didn't end well?" I asked Monique.

"There were stories, oui," she said.

"So, has he ever given any indication that he was interested in wanting to have sex with you later, after you turned him down in the beginning?"

"Absolutely not. I have not given him any reason to even think such a thing was possible as I have already said. I am gay and everyone knows this."

"But he does have liaisons with his dancers? Does that include the male dancers?" I asked.

"Oui. It is well known that he is bisexual."

"I see."

She shrugged and shook her head.

"Did you and Margo meet here?"

"Yes. I met her on my first day here. She helped me settle in," Monique said, looking at her lover with a warm smile.

"How soon did you two..."

"Almost at once," Margo said. "Something just seemed so right. I can't explain it."

"You don't need to," I said. "When magic happens, it happens."

"Absolutely," they said in unison, then started to giggle.

"Monique. Were you involved with anyone back in Montreal before you moved here?"

"No. Oh, I had a couple of girlfriends, yes, but nothing serious."

"Were they dancers as well?"

"Yes, some."

"Any of them want more than a casual friendship?"

"You mean a romantic relationship? No, I don't think so. At least, none that I was aware of," she said.

"Okay, I think that's it for now. Thanks for sharing with me and I'm happy that you're feeling a lot better," I said, standing up and putting on my hat.

"I am happy to help, especially, if it helps you catch this evil person," Monique said, as she and Margo walked me to the door.

"Enjoy your dinner. It smells great."

"Mon Dieu," she said, as she dashed back into the kitchen area.

Margo smiled at me as she slowly closed the door.

Later, at home, Jane and I sat on the couch watching television. It was running one of the new American game shows. All flash, pretty faces, and fake smiles. People will do anything it seems, to win something they really don't need. I have discovered these shows bring out the cynic in me.

"So, how did your meeting go with the Levesque girl?" Jane asked from the comfort of my arm that held her.

"Interesting. It always surprises me just how much unconventional sexual activity goes on in the art community," I said.

"How so?"

"You remember that case from a year back with that young woman killing those male actors?" I felt her head nod.

"Well, there was a lot of sexual experimentation going on, you know, men with men, women with women. Even the girl that I shot had a screwed up sexual history. Gabe once told me that it has always been there. It is only now that it's coming out into the light. No more hiding. Oh well, 'c'est la vie', as they say."

"Yes, but what about the case? Did she shed any new light at all?"

"Yeah, I think so. I've been thinking that something completely different may be going on. Something that doesn't involve the local dance community."

"Uh-huh?"

"I got a feeling that these troubles may have followed her here from Montreal."

"Really? How so?"

"Not sure yet."

She sat up and looked at me. "Oh you. You're such a tease."

"Sorry baby, but, you know I'll tell you just as soon as I figure out how to."

"Harrumph."

"C'mon baby, don't be like that. You know how I work," I said, lifting my arm for her to settle back in.

After a moment she smiled and said, "Sorry," then snuggled back down.

Ah...married life.

Chapter Fifteen

I called St. Jacques earlier and made arrangements for him to meet me. He said he could meet me at a bar near his place. I got there fifteen minutes ahead of the scheduled time.

I went inside and found a small table in a quiet corner and sat down, When the waitress arrived, I ordered an espresso coffee. The place was half empty. There was a radio behind the cashier's station set to a popular music station. It was playing one of the current protest songs by Bob Dylan that was currently going around. I sort of liked it, being a pacifist by nature, and believing the war in Asia made no sense.

St. Jacques arrived five minutes late. He wore the same tan jacket from a few days ago. Today he had a long scarf loosely wrapped around his neck with the ends hanging down below his waist. He also wore a black beret cantered to one side. Very continental. Very chic. Very artsy.

He spotted me and made his way across the room. He moved with an air of arrogant indifference yet, he still took note of who was watching him as he made his entrance;

especially the few women who were definitely eyeing him.

"Monsieur Murphy," he said, offering a hand as he sat down. I accepted it without standing.

"Thanks for seeing me on such short notice," I said.

"As you say, no problem," he said, crossing his legs.

Just then the waitress arrived carrying a glass of red wine and setting it down in front of him. I didn't see him order when he came in. He must come here often, I reckoned, and that was his usual order.

"Merci, mon cher," he said, looking up at her and smiling. The girl smiled back then looked at me.

"Anything else, sir?"

"No thanks. I'm good."

"So? What can I do for you?" St. Jacques asked, picking up the glass.

"I'm hoping you can shed a little light on something for me."

"Such as?"

"I'm curious. How did you come to know Monique Levesque?"

"Ah. She was dancing at a studio owned by one of my former teachers. I was visiting one day about a year ago to discuss certain technical aspects of a dance I was choreographing. I happen to see her rehearsing a movement from Swan Lake and was impressed with her interpretation and understanding of the movement."

"Um, I see," I said, not understanding what the hell he was talking about, but pushed on nonetheless. "And...?"

"Yes, well, I started to follow her career more closely with the idea of finding a role for which she would be best suited. I decided on her as my choice to lead my newest production after watching her dance at an exhibition."

"As a choreographer, do you have your own studio?"

"No. Usually, I choose a studio to perform my dances," he said.

"So, you don't use the same studio then?"

"The studio is selected based on the style of dance I require."

"Does that mean you use different dancers as leads from these studios or do you use the same dancers?"

"It varies of course, but, yes, I tend to work with the same core group of dancers when possible."

"And Monique is one of these I take it?"

"Yes, but not initially. I made her a part of the group just recently."

"How many other female dancers do you use regularly as your leads?"

"I usually work with only one lead, the prima ballerina."

"Who were the others? For example, who was your last one?"

"Why do you ask?" He placed his glass on the table and pulled out a pack of Export

'A' cigarettes. He offered me one which I declined. He flipped open a Zippo and lit up.

"No particular reason, just asking questions. That's what detectives do; ask a lot of questions. See what comes to the surface," I said.

He gave me a quizzical look.

"Sorry. We ask a lot of questions and hope that answers give a hint where to go next."

"Ah, yes, I see...I think."

"Anyway, back to the question. How come you didn't use her?"

"She left abruptly. Now Monique was my only choice."

"I don't suppose you could tell me her name?"

"Julia Dion, if you must know."

"Thanks."

"Is this all?"

"Just one more thing. Can you give me the address of Monique's former studio?"

He gave me the address which I wrote in my notebook.

"Why do you ask these questions about Montreal? Surely you cannot be suggesting...?"

"Just exploring every avenue for possible connections," I said.

"Absurd. There can be no connection there. Impossible."

"Maybe. But I still have to look," I said.

I stood and dropped a couple of dollars on the table for the coffee, and a tip. I stuck out my hand which he accepted and said thanks again.

Julia Dion. I wondered if she was the one that left the companyunder a cloud and pregnant?

I left thinking if it possible that this Julia Dion had followed Levesque to Toronto? One way to find out; call the studio in Montreal and try and find her. This was a good job for Maddie. She had a talent for rooting out information.

When I got back to the office, I found a handwritten note on my desk from Maddie.

'HAVE GONE TO RELIEVE ERNIE AT THE STUDIO. M.'

I tossed the note in the trash can and sat down. I reached for a piece of paper and jotted down my instructions for her to take of tomorrow and put it on her desk. Then I got up and headed for home, locking the door as I left.

The next morning, after I dropped Jane off at the library, I headed over to Smithson's studio. It was time to bring her up to date on where I was with this case. She was paying the bill after all, besides, I figured she'd want to know that the troubles at the studio were likely over since, whoever was doing these things, had taken it outside the studio. I chalked this up to the high visibility of the men I hired to watch over the studio. Too risky for this person to press their case against Levesque there.

I arrived around ten-thirty. The place was fairly empty as the dancers and students hadn't shown up yet. I saw another man standing inside the main dance area looking bored. I went over to him.

"Mornin'," I said. "You must be one of Ernie's mates?"

I offered my hand which he accepted. He looked to be about fifty or so. He wore a loose fitting jacket over a solidly built body. He looked like a linebacker. I figured he was carrying a gun under the jacket hence the loose fit. He carried himself comfortably, relaxed but ready to react. Ernie made a good pick.

"Yep. You Murphy?"

"Yeah, and it's Murph," I said, shaking his extended hand.

He nodded. "Mel. Melvin Jackson."

"Getting bored?"

"Yeah, a little. Scenery's nice though, even if it is a bit airy fairy, if ya get me."

"Uh-huh. Imagine it would be," I said.

"Any idea how much longer this gig'll last?"

"I think I'll be pulling you guys off this place today but, I might keep you on another couple of days for some bodyguard work. Up for that?"

"Cool."

"Great. I'll let Ernie know. See ya," I said and headed for the office.

"Come in," Adele said in response to my knock.

I opened the door and went in. She was sitting behind her desk as usual with a small pile of mail in front of her. I didn't know how she sis it, but she looked lovely as usual dressed in a stylish two piece pale purple suit with a frilly blouse underneath.

"Am I interrupting anything?" I asked, closing the door.

"No, not really. Just part of my morning routine," she said, pushing the letters to the side. "Please." She gestured to one of the chairs in front of her desk.

"I thought it was time to report on my progress."

"Are you any closer to finding out what's been going on or who's doing these things?"

"I think so, yeah. At least I now have a working theory."

"A theory?"

"Yeah. I think we can eliminate the other studios and outside dancers. From what I've been able to determine, it just doesn't add up that your troubles came from there.

"Does this mean it's over?"

"Not quite, but I think it's safe to say that you shouldn't expect any more mysterious 'accidents' around your studio. I think it's also safe to say that your studio was never the intended target. It was simply a convenient place to try and get at the target. Understand?"

"Target? What do you mean? Who...?"

"I think it's either Monique or St. Jacques, or even both," I said. "In any event, any further attempts or incidents won't likely happen here."

"I'm so happy to hear that. I've been so worried about my dancers being injured. But, you said Monique or Pierre were the intended targets. Is she in any kind of danger?"

"There is still someone out there. I think it's possible that the person I'm looking for may have followed them from Montreal."

"Really?"

"It's a working theory," I said, nodding. "I don't suppose you've heard of, or know anything about, this Gaudet Studio?"

"Only that it is highly regarded in our circles."

"St. Jacques seems to think so to, since he was once a student of the owner."

"Yes, I knew that," she said.

"By the way, besides his reputation as a choreographer, do you know anything else about him?"

"Like what?"

"I understand that he seems to become involved with his dancers on a sexual level, that sort of thing."

"Well, this is a very free spirited group of people. Highly emotional and very sensual. They have to be in order to be good dancers. It's the connection with music, you see. Unlike singers who can express their feelings through the music with words, dancers interpret the music through and with their bodies. This is a greater, deeper expression and their movements becomes a language of its own. Do you understand?”

“Yes, actually, I do.”

She smiled at me.

“However, I can say that I have not heard that he's involved with anyone in particular since he arrived here.”

I raised an eyebrow.

“Heh, heh. It's a small and intimate community, Mr. Murphy.”

“Oh. Right,” I said. “Well, anyway. I think I'll be pulling the men I hired from the studio so, you can get back to business as usual.”

She looked a little concerned for a brief moment. “What if...?”

“I'm pretty sure that there won't be any more incidents, but if there is, I'll have someone here very quickly.”

“Okay. That'll be fine and thank you.”

“You're welcome. But the job isn't done yet. There's still the business of protecting Monique. I take it you want me to continue?”

“Oh yes, absolutely.”

“Good. She's a great young woman. Lots of character. Don't worry too much. This business will be over soon,” I said, hoping to reassure her.

“I hope so.”

Chapter Sixteen

I stopped at a deli on the way back to office and picked up a pastrami on rye with hot mustard, brown sauerkraut, and a couple of Kosher dill pickles. One of my favorite lunches. I got to the office around twelve. Maddie was out, probably getting lunch. When I sat down, I saw the little red light blinking on the answering machine.

There were three messages.

The first message was from Gus Ferguson, a detective friend of Abe and me, the second from Ernie asking me to call him. He left a number. The third was from one of my regular clients asking if I was available yet to take on an assignment.

I called the last first and explained that I was still unavailable for a few more days and referred him to another agency that I used when I was busy.

I called Ernie next. He had talked with Mel Jackson and heard that I was pulling the detail from the studio. I confirmed this but told him to keep one of his guys around for another couple of days to keep an eye on the girl. He said he would keep Mel and then asked when he could expect payment. I told him I'd have something no later than tomorrow.

My last call was to Gus.

"Hey, what's up?" I asked when he came online.

"Someone took a run at Pierre St. Jacques last night."

"What?"

"Yeah. He took one in the arm. He was taken to emergency."

"Christ. When did this happen?"

"Around midnight. He was coming out of a club with several other people when someone drove by and fired a single shot. Looks like the shooter used a twenty-two."

"How bad was he hurt?"

"He's okay. The bullet caught him in the arm. Looks like it might just be a flesh wound. He was lucky."

"You said someone drove by?"

"Yeah. Near's anyone remembers, it was a late model Ford or Chev. Two toned. Looks like only one person inside. Must've slowed down and fired through the passenger's window."

"Or someone in the rear, hunched own," I suggested.

"Or that," he said with a hint of sarcasm.

"Did anyone see if it was a man or woman?"

"Mixed opinions" he said.

"Anyone else hurt?"

"Yeah. one other. A bystander. Dead."

"Jesus," I said.

"Thought you'd want to know since he's mixed up with what you're working on, which by the way, I'll need to talk to you about now."

"Yeah. Yeah, sure. Want me to come in?"

"Yeah, keep it official, but there's no rush. Get here when you can, but today would be nice."

"Okay. I'll be over before the end of the day and thanks for the call. Appreciate it," I said then hung up.

Just when I thought I was getting a handle on the case, someone threw a monkey wrench into the works. I had just about decided that Monique Levesque was the intended target, and everything that happened so far was an attempt to sabotage St. Jacques' production by intimidating his lead dancer. But now? There was definitely something more sinister in this than I thought. I wondered if this tied in with what I'd been thinking regarding a Montreal connection.

I could see the things that had happened starting to make some sort of sense, if someone felt rejected or whatever. However, this attempt on St. Jacques' life was a major escalation by whoever was behind this. They clearly wanted to do more than screw up St. Jacques' production.

There was nothing to be gained by canceling his ticket. The smart play would be to get rid of the girl and cut Smithson out of the running. Anything else was shooting yourself in the foot, no pun intended. Had to be something else. Something personal. If it was personal, then Levesque was out of the line of fire.

The more I thought about what I knew so far, the more it looked unlikely that the one I was after was a local.

I arrived at the police station around two-forty-five. It was a typical day at the station. Busy.

Cops and civilians crowded the main room with a half dozen or so in front of the duty desk. I recognized the duty constable and tossed him a wave as I approached the counter.

"Hi Larry," I said.

"Murph," he said when he looked at me. "Long time no see. What's up?"

"Here to see Gus. He's expecting me."

"Yeah, he left word you'd be droppin' in. How's Jane by the way? Still puttin' up with ya?"

"Everybody's a comedian these days," I said with a smile. "She's good."

He reached for his phone and dialed four numbers.

"Murph's here," he said into the mouthpiece. After a moment or two, he hung up. "You know the way. Tell Jane I said hi."

"You bet, thanks."

I headed for the stairs that went up to the second floor and the Homicide squad room. The squad room was busy. Detectives were taking statements or finishing their filing for the day. This was the part of the job the public never sees or thinks about. Desks were shared by the different shifts.

I caught a glimpse of Gerry Epstein, a local hustler I knew who worked the Village, was sitting at Bill Jebson's desk when I stepped inside.

"Hey Gerry, long time no see," I said. "Being a bad boy again?" I said when I reached Gus' desk.

"Murph. Hey, what can I say, ya know me, ain't done nothin'." he said, looking up at me.

"Good luck selling that."

"Thanks," he said. "Hey, man, sorry ta hear what happened to Pete."

"Yeah. If you're outta here, his funeral is this Saturday." I gave him the name of the cemetery.

"Hey Bill," I said, looking at the detective. What's shaking?"

"Same old shit jus' higher," he said, nodding at Epstein.

"That's why you get the big bucks," I said with a chuckle. "By the way, how's Rachel?" Rachel was his wife.

"Good. Pregnant. Again."

"No shit. What's that now? Three?"

"Four," he said with a smile. "Reason for the third trip at bat."

He has been trying to make sergeant for over a year.

"That's great man. And good luck, I mean it. I really hope you nail it this time."

"Thanks, Murph. You here to see Abe?"

"No. Gus."

"He just stepped away for a moment. Go ahead an' take a seat." he said, as he tilted his chin towards Gus's desk.

I stepped over and knocked twice on the glass panel.

"Yeah?"

I opened the door and went in.

Gus came back a few minutes later and took his seat.

"Hear anything more from the hospital?" I asked once he settled in.

"St. Jacques was released with only a few stitches."

"That's something anyway."

"Okay. So talk. What the hell's going on?"

"You already know most of it."

I proceeded to fill him in on everything I had so far, including the theory about a Montreal connection.

"Up to now, I've been working on the idea that someone was trying to scare the girl off, maybe even back to Montreal. That would leave Smithson without a dancer that St. Jacques would accept with the result that she would lose the deal. The only other studio in contention with an acceptable lead dancer is Zola's. That and another dance studio up near Scarborough. With me so far?" I asked.

He nodded.

"Well, after checking into this studio, I'm satisfied that everything is kosher with them. I had one other possibility to follow up on. A dancer named Olivia DeMarco. She was with Zola's originally but left for Smithson's studio shortly after St. Jacques gave the deal to Smithson. I figured her for the best candidate for the things happening to Levesque hoping to take her place if she succeeded. But that didn't pan out either. So, I got to thinking, what if the problem wasn't local? What if it followed the girl here from Montreal?"

"Interesting," Abe said. "So, what did you learn?"

"Nothing yet. I just got this idea yesterday. I'm looking into some lines of interest as we speak."

"Hmm. You think this is connected?"

"Yeah, I think so. Although, it doesn't make sense."

"Whaddya mean?"

"Well, if everything that's happened so far has been to scare off the girl and torpedo Smithson's studio in order to step in as the replacement, then it makes no sense whatever to take St. Jacques out, right?"

"Would appear to be counterproductive, yeah," Gus said. "So, what now?"

"Montreal. I think the answers might be there."

"Yeah, well, keep me posted, okay?"

"You bet."

Now, what's going on with Crazy Pete's killing?"

"Only what Abe has probably passed on to you. I got some ideas and have people keeping an eye out. If they come back, I'll know."

"Then what?"

"Then they're all yours...after I have a short 'instructional' chat with the shooter."

"I'll pretend I didn't hear that," he said. "Okay. Thanks for coming in. We'll talk again when you have something."

I decided to stop off at Ed's Pool Hall and see how things were progressing with finding the kids that killed Pete. I hadn't heard from him for a while.

He was sitting where he usually did, at the end of the bar near the back reading the paper, probably the racing stats. No one was playing on the table that was Pete's usual spot where he hustled his pigeons. Ed had placed an empty beer glass on the high table in the corner and strung two strips of black cloth crossed over it. That was where Pete usually sat.

I looked around the room. About a half dozen people were sitting around nursing a drink. Two of the other pool tables had games going on.

"Yo, Murph. What's shakin'?" One of the patrons said as I walked by. His name was Jenkins. A dock worker and sometime street muscle used by a local loan shark. I did him a favor a while back at Pete's request. Wasn't much, but he still remembered.

"Wally," I said. "How's it going?"

"It's goin'."

"Good to hear."

Ed had got up and poured a Budweiser draft from the tap and set in on the bar.

"What's new?" I asked, sitting on a stool.

"Nothin'. The fuckers gone ta ground."

I got to thinking that the reason we haven't found this guy yet was because, if he was a student, it was Spring Break and maybe he was out of town.

"Don't worry about it. I got an idea to flush him out. Can you pass the word that there's a new shooter in town looking to score a name for himself. Drop the word that he's got a good size bankroll to play with. Then keep your ears open and call me when they surface." I picked up the glass and took a long pull of the cold beer.

"Sounds like that'd work. Should I call even if it's late?"

"Yeah. I don't care what time it is. You got my home number."

We talked about a few more things, mostly Pete and his burial. He again said thanks for the money that Pete left him. I didn't tell him he got it all. He didn't need to know.

I went outside and got in the car and went home.

* * *

Saturday dawned overcast and dreary. I stood at the window with a cup of coffee looking down into the street. People were going about their day like always, unaware of anything outside their little world. Christ, I thought, I felt maudlin this morning. At least it fit the day. Why is it that when you bury someone it's usually on a day like this.

"A penny for your thoughts," Jane said, as she came up behind me and put her arms around me.

"Ain't worth that much," I said.

"It's the funeral, isn't it?"

"Yeah, I guess so. Ever wonder why it always seems to be a day like this whenever there's a funeral. Why can't we send someone off under a bright sunny day?"

"Mmm. You really are in a mood, aren't you," she said, turning me away from the window and throwing her arms around my neck. "Kiss me."

I looked down into her beautiful face and smiled then lowered my lips to hers.

Forty minutes later, I rolled out of bed and headed for the shower. I emerged after ten minutes feeling renewed. She could really kick start the day, I thought, remembering. I went into the bedroom and started to dress. Jane padded off barefoot and naked to the bathroom to get ready. How I loved watching her body.

"Do you think there will be anyone else there?" she asked, as we drove to the cemetery.

"Don't know," I said. "Be nice if there are."

"How are things going on finding the ones who killed him?"

"Slow. They haven't been around much. But I'm working an angle that might lure them out."

"Uh-oh," she said.

"What's uh-oh?"

"Nothing."

"Come on, what's going on inside that pretty head of yours?"

"Usually when you say you've got a plan it means someone gets hurt."

"Not always," I said, as we pulled up to a red light. "Besides, it'll be up to them if it goes that way. And, if it does, then it won't be me that gets hurt."

"I know. I just worry," she said, placing a hand on my leg.

"It's like I always tell you, when one goes into a situation ready for trouble then they usually are the one with the control. Besides, I'll have a trick or two up my sleeve."

"You usually do."

We arrived at a small cemetery. It was a privately run non-denominational cemetery on an acre of land located in one of city's neighbourhoods. There were quite a number of markers in the ground and a work shed off in a corner. A small stone chapel was situated in the middle.

I had made arrangements for Pete to be cremated. Jane and I got out and made our way between the markers and headstones to where two men in black overcoats stood near a small mound of dirt; one holding an urn, I spotted Ed standing with a half dozen other men. They each wore a black band on their left arms.

I nodded at Ed when we got there. I recognized two of the six men as regulars from his bar. Jane stepped up and placed the floral bouquet she picked up on the way. I looked down at the small hole and saw the stone plaque which I ordered. It had Pete's name and particulars carved into it. Lying on the grass above it was a large bundle of flowers tied with a black ribbon. I cast a quick look at one of the two men.

He stepped over and passed me a small envelope. Inside was a sympathy card from his ex-wife.

"Shouldn't somebody say somethin?" Ed said to no one in particular.

"Yeah, I suppose something should be said," I answered.

Ed nodded and stepped forward a step.

"Well, what can you say about Pete? Let's face it, he wasn't exactly whatcha'd call a stand up citizen. But he was my friend. He never did me wrong. I'll miss him." Finished, he stepped back. A few of the other men stood listening and nodded.

I stepped forward and said, "Pete was my friend too. There was much we didn't know about him. Things he probably would never have shared. Once, in another life, he'd had a wife and two children. He had a career, a home. Then suddenly, his life changed, and he somehow ended up here, becoming the Pete we all knew." I paused for a moment.

"What happened to him was unfair and, as a farewell to him, I'm going to find the ones that did this and settle the score for him."

Ed and the others all slowly nodded.

I could think of nothing else to say, so I stepped back where Jane took my arm.

As we all headed away from the grave site, Ed came up beside me.

"Those was good words you said, thanks. I couldn't think of anything else to say, I mean it was 'Crazy' Pete after all, right?"

I nodded. "What you said was good, Ed. Pete wouldn't expect much more. It wasn't his style."

"You got that straight. Well, I'm off. Good day, Mrs."

Looking back at me, he said, "It's set up and I got everythin' in motion. I'll be in touch."

"My, but you do know some interesting people," she said, as we watched him walk away.

"Hmm. Maybe I ought to write a book. Call it, 'Village Characters' or something like that."

“Not a bad idea,” she said.

“Ha. Me a writer. Now there's a thought,” I said chuckling.

It was still early, and the weather didn't look like it was about get better any time soon, so I suggested that we spend the rest of the day taking in the action over in Markham, then later, head to the Village for something to eat then a show. I just didn’t want to sit at home; not today.

“Let's,” she said, as we arrived back at the car.

Chapter Eighteen

It was Monday morning. I decided it was time for a quick chat with Gus to fill him in on my plan to smoke out Pete's killer. I stopped off at a deli and picked up a couple of bagels with cream cheese and strips of lox, as well as two cups of coffee.

"Hey buddy," I said when I reached his desk and sat down, setting a coffee and the bag with the bagels on the desk.

"What's this?"

"Thought I'd check in and let you know what's shakin' like you asked," I said.

"That's good of you. The police always appreciate a good civic minded citizen, especially ones bearing gifts."

"Snarky bastard. What's got you in a mood so early in the day?"

"Mike's been ridin' my ass. Sorry didn't mean to crap on you," he said. "So, really, what's up?" He was referring to Captain Mike Franklyn, head of the detective division. He was my boss a lifetime ago when I wore the blue uniform.

"Here. Maybe this'll take the edge off the sting," I said, tearing the bag open and taking out the bagels. "You making any headway on Pete's murder?" I asked, handing him one of the bagels.

"Thanks. Not much. We're looking into your idea about the kids but, nothing so far. Why? You catch anything?"

"No, but I'm cooking up something," I said.

"Yeah? Like what?"

"A little bait and catch."

"Or, as we professionals say, entrapment."

"Hey, a rose by any other name..., besides, it isn't entrapment if I do it."

"Good point. Whaddya cooking up?"

"I got Ed spreading the word that an out of town stick with a roll is trolling the pool halls looking to score. I'm hoping this kid's ego is as big as I think it is. If he and his friends bite, Ed'll let me know and we'll set it up with me being the hustler. Then I'll call you and you can send one of the boys over and make the bust."

"On what basis?"

"Two things. Both circumstantial, I know, but strong, nonetheless. First, is Pete's wallet. I'm counting on this kid's ego again to have kept it as a trophy. Second, Ed can make the I.D. that he was the one Pete played last before leaving the bar."

"Okay. Say we arrest him and the others, so what? I still got nothing to take to the Crown."

"I bet if you can get them into the station and separate them, one or more of his buddies will crack without too much pressure."

"Hmm. Maybe. If they don't lawyer up first."

"Simple. Don't charge them right off. Bring them in for questioning. You know the routine."

"Okay. I'm in. Anything else on your mind?"

"Yeah. I pretty much figure that all this crap that's been happening with these dancers originated out of town, namely, in Montreal like I already said. I got a feeling that it's tied to the Levesque girl and St. Jacques. If the shooting is any indication, then I'd say more to him than her."

"Yeah, and..."

"I learned there's woman who danced for him that he had an affair with and it ended badly; very badly, according to what I've been told. There's even talk about a pregnancy and abortion. I managed to get her name and put Maddie on it. Meanwhile, I thought I'd call the studio in Montreal where she and St. Jacques spent their time together; see what I can dig up. Be interesting to see if she's still there or gone away."

"Away as in here."

"You got it. Then I'll try to find her. I figure between you and me we can locate her if she's in Toronto."

"Optimistic."

"Yep. That's me. Be nice to close this one quick. Might get Mike off your back for a while."

"Something else you learned from the detective manual you got out of the Cracker Jack box?" he said sarcastically.

"How'd ya know? You can borrow it anytime. Well, that's all I got for now."

"Okay. Thanks for the heads up, and this," he said, indicating the bagel and coffee. "Good luck. Watch your back."

"Always," I said, then stood up and left.

Back at my office, I dialed the long distance operator and asked for the phone number for the Gaudet Studio in Montreal.

Once I got through, I introduced myself to the girl on the other end and asked if I could speak with Mr. Gaudet. She said that he was not in and instead put me through to the studio's manager, Kevin Jameson.

"This is Kevin Jameson," said the voice on the other end of the phone.

He had a strong and slightly deep tone More...masculine.

"Morning," I said. "Thanks for taking my call."

"No problem. My day hasn't become too busy yet. I understand that you're a detective calling from Toronto?"

"That's correct," I said.

"How can I help?"

"I'm making inquiries concerning a case I'm working that involves ballet dancers. In the course of my investigation two names came up, and these people were connected to your studio."

"Oh my God, who?"

"Julia Dion and Monique Levesque."

"Yes, these girls danced here. They were two of our best. But I don't understand how they could possibly be connected to an investigation in Toronto. How did you acquire their names, if I can ask?"

"Pierre St. Jacques," I said, fudging the truth a little.

"Pierre? My God, is he involved in something?"

"There's been an incident involving him, yes," I said.

"What happened?"

"Sorry. I'm not at liberty to discuss that but, I can say he's okay. Now the girls. I know Miss Levesque is here but, I have not been able to find Miss Dion. Can you tell me if she is there?"

"Here? You mean here with the company? Now?"

"Yes."

"Well, uh, no," he stammered. "The last I heard St. Jacques picked Monique for his new show and she left for Toronto after he made his choice of a dance company. As for Dion, she left our company several months ago. It was sudden, as I recall, and under a cloud."

"Can you elaborate on what you mean by a 'cloud'?"

"Well, there were rumours that she and St. Jacques were involved beyond the dance. Something changed and he grew more dissatisfied with her, resulting in his breaking it off with her."

Bingo, I thought.

"Would be an imposition if I asked you to do me a favour?" I asked.

"I suppose so, depending on what is involved, that is."

"Nothing complicated. I would like to know if Miss Dion is still in Montreal? It would save me a trip."

"Yes, I can look into that," he said. "Just leave me your number where I can call back."

"Thank you. Oh, if you call, reverse the charges." I gave him my office number and Maddie's name.

"Okay, thanks again. I think that about covers everything I needed. You've been a big help. Oh, by the way, would it be possible to send me a picture of Dion?"

"Yes, I suppose so. I'm sure we still have some promotional shots on file. Where should I send them?"

I gave him my office address. I asked if he knew whether or not UPS had an office in Montreal, turns out they did. I suggested he send them with UPS, collect. He agreed and added, he would send them immediately. Great. I'd have them by tomorrow. I said thanks again and was about to hung up.

"Wait. What about Pierre? My God, he's our best..."

"Like I said, I can't discuss this but, I can tell you he is okay and working on his production. That's all I can say, sorry. Thanks again," I said then hung up.

Julia Dion. Now all I needed to do was find her.

It was almost twenty-past-one when I arrived at Smithson's studio. It was crowded with dancers of all ages milling about talking, laughing, dancing. I tended to forgot that she ran a teaching studio.

There was one class with a dozen or so people in it. They were a mixed bag of men and women, mostly women. It looked like they were doing some sort of social dancing.

"We offer a special dance class from noon to one-thirty to the general public. You know, anyone wanting to learn how to dance or to bone up on the latest steps," Adele said from behind me. I picked up the scent of her perfume which was wonderful.

"Good to know," I said. "I stay on this case long enough I might be tempted to take a lesson or two myself."

"I think you would be good," she said with a chuckle, as she stepped up beside me. "Are you here to see Monique?"

"Uh-huh, think she can spare me ten minutes?"

"That shouldn't be a problem. She's in practice room B down the hall."

"Thanks." I strode off down the hall.

AS I neared the door, I heard the sounds of classical music coming from behind it. I softly opened the door and stepped inside.

Monique was wearing form fitting black leotards with some sort of thick cloth that covered her lower legs; leg warmers, I think I was told. She wore a sleeveless skintight top that was tucked into the leotard and accented her small breasts perfectly. A thick terrycloth towel was draped around her neck. She had her hair tied in a bun on top of her head.

"Oh, hello," she said, panting slightly.

"Hi," I said. "It's good to see you working. I was hoping you could spare me a few minutes for some question?"

"Certainly. We can talk here, no one will interrupt us. I have the room until two o'clock for practice, if you wish."

There were three metal chairs in the room against one wall. She walked over to them; I followed behind enjoying the view.

"What is it that you wish to discuss with me?"

"While you were in Montreal, did you ever meet Julia Dion?"

"Of course. She was permanent members of the Gaudet Company, and the dancer Pierre always worked with the most, at least until that incident."

"Incident? Care to explain?"

"One day she comes into the studio and confronts Pierre. He takes her out of the room but, the shouting is loud. They said awful things to each other then she storms out and Pierre leaves a few minutes later."

"Did hear what they were fighting about?"

"Non, uh, no. but, it felt like it was extremely personal. Why do you ask?"

"My investigation is now leading me to believe there's a connection between Montreal and the attack on St. Jacques and yourself."

"Mon Dieu," she said. "So, these actions against me are..." she started to say.

"Collateral, I think everything that's been happening is actually directed against St. Jacques; aimed at hurting him. First, by going after the ballerina he chose as his primary dancer, then, failing that, going after him directly. How well did you know Julia Dion?"

"Not well. I had only come to Gaudet a short time before coming here. We met, of course. Pierre introduced us and told her I was to be his prima ballerina."

"And how did she react to that?"

"Okay, I think."

"Did you do anything with her while you were there?"

"I do not understand?"

"You know, socialize. Go out to parties. That sort of thing."

"No. Oh, we would be at the same clubs sometimes with the other dancers. But together? No. Whenever she was out she was almost always with her brother, Paul. The only time we would be together was when we danced or trained at the studio."

"So, it would be safe to say you weren't friends."

"Yes, that is correct. But I do not think we were enemies, either." She was quick to say.

"And you're sure that she showed no signs of resentment that you were picked by St. Jacques?"

"Yes, I am sure."

"Okay. That's about it for now, thanks, Oh yeah, one more thing, can you give me a general description of Dion?"

She proceeded to give me fairly good description which I jotted down in my notebook.

Julia Dion, twenty-four years old

Five-nine, one-hundred-ten pounds

Hair: Brunette, long,
Eyes: Blue

Liked to dress in gay bright colors, preferred modern styles,
i.e., mini skirts

Likes to flirt with men and has reputation as a tease

It wasn't a great list of identifying items, but at least I now had something to work with in trying to locate Julia Dion.

"You think that she is the one behind the things that have been happening, don't you?"

I looked at Monique sitting across from me with an expression that showed both concern and a little fear, perhaps. I decided to tell her the truth. Besides, if she knew, then she could be the look out and had a better chance of spotting Dion than I did.

"I don't know. But there is a possibility, yes," I said.

She sat back and nodded.

"I'm telling you this because I respect your courage and intelligence. Besides, you have the best chance of recognizing her if she does show herself and now that you know, you can better defend yourself."

"Merci," she said softly.

"But I must insist, if you do spot her, you're to contact me immediately or tell one of the men that I have guarding you. Agreed?"

"Okay."

"I mean this, Monique. If it is Dion, she has shown that she's dangerous and armed. She already killed one person, even if only by accident. Understand?"

"Yes," she said, nodding.

"Good. I really like you and think you are very brave young woman, and you have a great future ahead of you. Don't risk it."

"Thank you. I really do appreciate your caring and your opinion of me."

"Your welcome. Okay. I'm done here for now. I'll let you get back to your practice. We'll talk again soon."

I stood up and headed out of the office and back to the street where I flagged a cab and went back to the office.

Chapter Nineteen

On the way back to the office, I considered how I was going to find Julia Dion once I had her picture. It wouldn't be quite like looking for the proverbial needle in the haystack, close, but not entirely.

I had to assume that she would hole up somewhere in the Village area where she could blend in and maybe hook up easily with people who could help her lay low. Basically, hide in plain sight. The best place to do that was Rochdale College.

Rochdale College was an experiment based on the innovative idea of a free school; free admission, free choice of study area and so on. It was typical of the times. However, the reality of the place was that it had become a haven for drop-outs, runaways and drug dealers. Inhabited and controlled mostly by a biker gang that had more or less taken over the place.

Luckily, I had resources that could make searching a bit easier.

I also figured she would go to ground for a few days after the shooting. Let the heat cool down before her next move.

I still had no idea what was behind her actions: Was it anger over being passed over for the lead in this show? Or was it something else? Something personal involving St. Jacques? Maybe to do with the pregnancy and abortion rumours that kept popping up.

Great questions. Too bad I had no answers; hunches, yes but, no answers.

While I waited for the delivery from Montreal, I decided to call on St. Jacques again for another chat. This time about Dion. I asked the cabby to take me to St. Jacques' apartment instead of my office.

The doorman on the front desk dialed St. Jacques' room. He was in. He told me to go on up.

"Mr. Murphy," St. Jacques said, as he stood to the side of the open door. "Enter, please." I noted that his arm was in a sling.

I stepped in and went to one of the chairs and sat down.

"Drink? Coffee?" he offered, standing near the kitchen counter where a large carafe of coffee was sitting.

"Coffee. Black. Thanks," I said, putting my hat on the small coffee table. "How's the arm?"

"Sore," he said, "but, otherwise, alright."

St. Jacques poured two cups of coffee then came and placed them on the table and sat in the chair opposite me.

"How may I help you this time?" he asked.

"Julia Dion," I said.

"Ah yes. Very beautiful woman and superb dancer."

"Anything else?" I asked, picking up my cup and taking a sip. It was still hot and strong.

"Meaning?"

"Did she do more than dance for you?"

"You are very, um, direct, oui?"

I said nothing and waited.

After a moment, he relaxed and said, "You are correct in your assumption. There was more than dancing for me."

"I have heard that your relationship did not end well?"

"You are well informed."

"Apparently, it was a public break-up."

"Quite so," he said, picking up his cup. "Most unfortunate and regrettable."

"And the pregnancy?"

"Again, most regrettable. She, Julia, came to me demanding that I accept responsibility and to take appropriate steps. That was not possible, of course."

"Why?"

"It was understood when we began that it would be a physical relationship only. No emotional entanglements. She decided otherwise."

"Yes," I said. "Then what happened?"

"I had to end the relationship and, sadly, our collaboration," he said bluntly.

It was clear the man had no sense of responsibility for the consequences of his liaisons. Something inside me wanted to stand up and beat the crap out of him but I kept it down.

"So, it was your idea that she abort the pregnancy?"

"Yes, if she ever wanted to dance again."

It was getting harder to keep my temper in check.

"You must have been disappointed when Monique Levesque rejected your advances."

"Her tastes lay elsewhere, I'm afraid. A pity. She has such a beautiful body. Young and strong."

"But you chose her anyway," I said.

"But of course. Ballet and sex are two different things. I do not let one determine or influence the other."

"Do the women know that?"

"Of course. Why would they think otherwise? I gave no such reason to think it was more."

"Well, I have a feeling that there's one who would disagree."

"Really?" He actually was surprised by this observation. Amazing. He really did believe that a woman would be content with just having a sexual relationship with him. When in point of fact, he only saw them as a dancer and, maybe, an amusing diversion.

"And you think one of them is Julia?"

"I don't know, but it would explain a few things about what's been happening."

"Mon Dieu."

I decided to tell him so that he could be on his guard when alone.

"I am still not a hundred percent sure it's Dion but, if I were you, I'd take steps to cover yourself. Watch your back."

"I will," he said. "I still cannot believe what you have said. It is too wicked."

"In my line of work I have to look at all the things people don't want to see or admit to in order to make sense out of things. In this case, everything seems to point to someone looking to hurt your production and reputation, at least in the beginning. The 'accidents' at Smithson's studio were, I think, intended to either injure or frighten off the Levesque girl. When that failed, they raised the stakes and started to target her with more serious things, like the needles in her shoes, the attack in the washroom at the club; are you following any of this?"

"Oui," he said, nodding. He was looking at me intently.

"Anyway, Levesque turned out to be made of sterner stuff and refused to be intimidated. So, they had to raise the bar even higher. Go straight for the jugular. You."

"Moi?"

"It was no accident the other night. I believe you were the target."

"But why? It was only a sexual affair."

"As they say...'a woman scorned...," I said.

"I did not know," he said, sitting back with a bewildered look on his face. "You are certain of this?"

"No, but I recognize some of the signs. A while back I worked on a case involving another woman who had a misguided sense of love."

"And you think that this happening here?"

"Maybe. Some women think that when they give their body to someone, it is out of love and think it is a shared view. Let's face it, until recently, that's been the accepted way of things."

"I do not follow...until what?"

"You'd know better than I would."

"Ah, yes, I see. It is a time of change we live in."

"Anyway, I think that it might be a good idea for you to rethink your activities and keep a watchful eye open, like I said. If you do happen to spot her then you should call me or the police."

"The police?"

"That's right. Because there was a murder, they'll be treating this as a homicide. If you have to get in touch, call this number and ask for Detective Ferguson. Got it?" I gave him the phone number for the station.

"Oui. Yes. I understand and thank you."

"Okay. Well, I'll get out of your hair now. Good luck," I said, as I picked up my hat and headed for the door.

Chapter Twenty

I needed to clear my head of the bad vibes I was feeling after talking to St. Jacques. I'd come across some self-centered assholes in my life but this guy took the cake. And what truly pissed me off was how he was getting away with his treatment and attitudes towards women in this day of women's liberation. Being a genius is one thing, but what he did to the Dion woman was unforgivable.

This case was reviving the memory of an old case involving another young woman. I still had bad memories of the Lucy Addams affair. It ended with me having to kill a very young and unbalanced woman. The saddest part was she had been damaged by her own father and the effect of that betrayal led to her madness. Sometimes, the image of her sitting on the floor against the wall with part of her chest blown open from my shot, still haunted me.

"Is he in?" I asked one of the detectives who was sitting at a desk with two elderly people sitting in chairs talking to him. He looked up briefly and gave me a quick nod.

"Come," Abe said from behind the closed door after I rapped on the glass panel a couple of times.

He looked up from the open file in front of him when I stepped in, closing the door behind me. "What's up?" he asked.

"Got a few minutes for a friend?" I said, taking a seat in front of the desk.

Abe sat back and locked his fingers behind his head. "You bet. What's up?"

"It's this case. I just left St. Jacques, the choreographer. The guy's a really piece of shit."

Abe just quietly; waiting. He knew my moods, especially the ones where I needed to blow off some steam.

"You remember me saying, I thought things were looking like there was a connection to Montreal?"

He nodded.

"Well, I called the studio where the Levesque girl came from and where St. Jacques has a strong connection. I learned that he had another dancer named, Julia Dion that he worked with exclusively. Turns out, St. Jacques was hooked up sexually with her. Anyway, the long and short of it is that she got pregnant, and when she confronted him, he refused to take responsibility and told he that if she ever wanted to dance again, she had to get rid of it."

"Jesus. Did she?"

"I think so, yeah. Point is, I think she has decided to take her revenge on him for what he did."

"You got proof?"

"No, but everything I've put together supports the theory. I already had a talk with Gus about it."

"So, what's eatin' you?"

"The case made me remember Lucy Addams."

"Oh."

I didn't need to explain further, he understood. I have never forgiven completely myself for her death.

"Now you're thinkin' this Dion woman might be here to kill him an' if you get to her first it'll end like the Addams girl?"

I nodded.

"I don't want another ghost to carry around," I said, lowering my head.

"I know, but it's the job you chose to work. Bad shit happens sometimes, Matt. Look at Pete. None of this is your fault. You gotta move on. You ever talk to Jane 'bout any of this?'

I shook my head. "She worries enough whenever I take on a case. She doesn't need to add this to the load."

"You're not givin' her enough credit, buddy," he said, leaning forward. "She really loves you. You should think seriously about trustin' that love; trustin' her."

"You're right, I guess."

By the way, back to the case, has he made any advances to the Levesque girl?"

"No. She goes the other way exclusively."

"You sure 'bout that?"

"Uh-huh. In fact, she's living with one of Smithson's other dancers."

"Is that the Manson girl?"

Abe always had a steel trap memory. Once he put something in there, it was never far away, and he could recall a fact almost immediately. One of the things that made him a good detective.

"Yeah. Anyway, as I was saying, I called Montreal and spoke with the studio manager, a guy named, Kevin Jameson. He said St. Jacques had been working with Dion for some time. He also said he was sleeping with her. I asked him to send any photos he still had of her. He agreed to send them along. They're coming UPS and should be here by tomorrow. I'll get one to Gus when they get here."

"Okay, say this Dion is the one behind everything, including the shooting, how can you prove it? Let's face it, what you got so far wouldn't get Gus past the secretary at the Crown Attorney's office."

"I know. I didn't say I had the thing wrapped up with a bow on it. I'm just letting you in on what I have so far."

"'Appreciate it, but why're you so forthcoming? Usually, you play everything closer to the chest, and it's usually at the wire, when you give up everything."

I sat there quietly looking at my friend. There wasn't much to say; as I said before, he knows me too well.

"Yeah."

"Okay, Murph. Gotcha. Get that photo to him when you can and thanks for stoppin' in. Did it help?"

"Yeah," I said. "I don't feel like beating the crap out of some poor bastard anymore."

"So, why're you sticking with this case? It's pretty much over isn't it? I mean, you did what she hired you to do, solve the mystery of the accidents."

"It's more than that. Monique Levesque may still be in danger. Certainly, St. Jacques is. Smithson has asked me to stick around a while longer and look out for them."

"Yeah." he said, sitting forward.

"Ghosts can't hurt me," I said, standing up.

"True. But they can distract."

"I'm not too worried. I'm not the target."

"Not yet."

"Hey, that's what I got you for."

Abe slowly shook his head. "Oh, by the way, how're you doing on Pete's killer?"

"Nothing yet. The kid's gone to ground. No one has seen him and his crew lately. I'm not worried. He'll surface again. Kid can't help it. Ego's too big. I'm kind of hoping he thinks he untouchable."

"Well, keep in touch."

Once back on the street, I decided to head over and check in with Gabe before going home.

The club was quiet. I went to my usual booth by the kitchen door. I signaled one of the waitresses to bring a coffee as I walked across the floor. Gabe was behind the bar; I gave him a wave. He stopped what he was doing and joined me in the booth.

"Don't you ever go home? Seems whenever I come in here there you are," I said, as he settled in.

"What can I say. This is my baby," he said, smiling.

"Huh?" Hey. Sometimes some things do get by me.

"I bought an interest in the club. You're looking at a part owner."

"Wow. No shit! That's great, Gabe. I really mean that. You earned it."

"Thanks, Murph," he said, beaming.

"Thought I'd stop off for a coffee before heading home and check in."

"Not much to report, sorry. I heard about the shooting. I do hope St. Jacques is okay."

"Yeah. Just a flesh wound. Nothing serious."

"They know who did it?"

"Got some ideas. Listen, I'll be around tomorrow with some photos that I'll leave with you. You can share it around. If anyone sees this person or knows where I can find them tell them to call me or Gus Ferguson. You got his number."

"Certainly. Is this the person responsible...?"

"Let's say, it's a person of interest."

I finished my coffee and headed for home.

I was about halfway to my car which was parked around the corner on Lowther Avenue. The sidewalk was crowded as usual with kids mostly. I say kids when in fact they ranged from fifteen to thirty. As I squeezed through them, I was approached at least a dozen times by one of them for money. I spotted the corner just ahead when I heard someone call my name from across the street.

"Hey Murph," a man yelled. I barely heard him over the street noise. Then I spotted him as he stepped into the street and headed toward me.

I recognized him as John MacDonald, although everyone who knew him just called him Mac. He was a regular at Ed's place. I remembered seeing him at the funeral. Ed told me once that Mac was originally from somewhere down on the east coast, I think he said, Cape Breton. Came to Toronto looking for work but ended up hooking up with Pete and started running his own action with a couple of others.

"Mac," I said when he reached me. "What's up?"

He sidled up close to me. "Over here." He pushed his way past a half dozen men and women to a narrow alley. I followed behind.

"Heard yer lookin' fer them kids that did ole Pete," he said once we out of the traffic.

"That's right," I said. "You got something?"

"Yeah, think so. Ed put da word out there's hot shooter in town lookin' fer some action. A cuppla mates of mine tells me there's a kid askin' round lookin' to find this guy."

"Yeah? When was this and where?"

"Last night."

He mentioned the names of a couple of taverns, some I knew, others not so much.

"Anyway, I tell Ed an' he sez if I see you to tell ya. He also tole me an' some a da other guys to spread da word the shooter might be at da Derby tomorrow night 'round ten."

I knew about the Derby. A small local tavern down on Selby Street which was not that far from the Scarborough area.

"Okay, thanks," I said and fished out a sawbuck and offered it to him.

He declined saying, "Not dis time. Dis one is for Pete. Ya needed any of us to back ya up?"

"No. I got this," I said, putting the banknote back in my pocket. "Thanks. Tell Ed I'll be by to let him know how it ended."

"Okay. Jus' make sure ya cut da pricks a new one."

"Count on it." I headed out of the alley for my car.

Jane had arrived home early and started dinner. I could smell the aroma of roast chicken as I walked down the hall to the door of our apartment. It was nice having this to come home to every day, I thought, as I rapped twice on the door to let her know it was me. It was our private signal.

She was in the kitchen standing at the counter. She had changed into a comfortable pair of flat shoes she liked to wear and blue Capri pants with a short apron around her waist, and a loose white blouse. She had her hair tied back in a ponytail with a ribbon.

"Hi, baby," I said, as I wrapped my arms around her waist and nuzzled her neck.

"Hi yourself," she said, tilting her head slightly to give me more of her neck to kiss. "Dinner's almost ready. You got time to clean up and change if you want."

"Well, if there's that much time…"

"Oh you," she giggled. "I married a sex addict."

"Is that a complaint?"

"Never. But we don't have that much time. Everything is almost done." She wiggled out of my arms and went to the stove.

"Damn," I said.

"Don't pout," she said, as she came back with the chicken from the oven. "You can carve if you're not going to change."

"Okay. Okay, you win. I'll go clean up. But I'm going to want a rain check."

"Hoped you'd ask," she said with that little suggestive smile she always used.

"Be back in a minute."

Later, as we sat on the couch enjoying the last of the wine and listening to the news, she asked, "Making any progress on the case?"

"Some. Should go a bit better and quicker once I have the photos from Montreal, or at least I hope so," I said. I had filled her in on my calls to Montreal and what I was thinking.

"You're pretty sure it's her then?"

"Everything points that way, yeah. Why? You thinking I missed something?"

"No. Not really."

"Maddie found out that Dion has been away from the studio for about the same amount of time as everything that's been happening. Makes her a very strong suspect."

"I know. I'm not saying she isn't. It's just that, speaking as a woman, there must be something else besides being upset over a break-up."

"So, you're saying that she would have begun to think of St. Jacques in a romantic sense?"

"Maybe not quite romantically, but certainly as more than an occasional encounter."

"Even in that world they live in? Don't forget, it's pretty loose in terms of conventional morality. The usual constraints don't apply, especially when it comes to sex. I mean, look at Levesque. And remember what it was like back during the Addams case."

"Yes, I know. But I think that deep down most women will, at some level, expect or assume, that once they give their body to a man it implies a meaningful relationship."

"Damn," I said. "You never fail to impress me with how smart you are, even if what you say would cause the libbers to come looking for your head."

"That's one of the reasons why I married you...my protector." She leaned in and kissed me on the cheek.

"Well, most women would be hurt, of course being thrown over by someone she believed she was in love with, right?"

"True, but we get over that fairly quickly. No. I think this Dion woman must be seeking revenge for something else. Definitely. The only thing that might drive her to the actions she's taken might be the pregnancy and, didn't you say there was also rumours of an abortion?"

"Makes sense when you say it like that," I said.

"You're welcome," Jane said.

I grabbed her to me and gave her a big kiss. "Maybe you should be a detective."

"No, thank you. I'm quite happy being married to one. Now, for my reward. I want you to exercise those marvelous muscles of yours and carry me into the bedroom where you can show me your appreciation."

"Done." I stood and scooped her up into my arms and headed down the hall to the bedroom as she started kissing my neck.

Chapter Twenty-One

The first order of business when I arrived at the office in the morning was another call to Kevin Jameson in Montreal.

"Kevin Jameson," he said, when he answered.

"Mr. Jameson. It's Matt Murphy calling again from Toronto."

"The detective, yes, I remember."

"Have you a few minutes to spare for a couple more questions?"

"Yes, what would you like to know?"

"I understand that you spoke with my assistant yesterday."

"That's right. I passed along the information you asked to me to find."

"Yes, she told me, thanks for that by the way."

"Actually, it wasn't that hard to get."

"Oh?"

"Yes. I lucked out on my first call. It was to a girlfriend of hers, not one of the dancers. She told me that Julia hasn't been well, not since the break-up with St. Jacques. In fact, she said that she hasn't even been dancing either."

"Did she say if she was still in Montreal?"

"No. She and her brother, Paul, have been away. Although, she has come back for a day or two."

"Did she say when they left?"

"About seven or eight weeks ago."

"Would it be possible to get her friend's name and phone number?" I asked.

"I suppose so." He gave me her name, address, and phone number which I jotted in my notebook.

"I really appreciate everything you done for me."

"Not a problem. I hope it helps with your case."

"Thanks, good-bye."

"Au revoir," he said then the line went dead, and I hung up.

My next call was to the railway and bus companies. Turned out that there was a regular daily service running between Montreal and Toronto York on both.

I needed a drink just like any hard-boiled P.I. would do, but instead, I opted for a coffee and a ham and cheese sandwich. The hot mustard would make it a tough guy lunch.

When I returned to the office after a quick lunch, I found a large envelope with the UPS stamp had been pushed under the door. The pictures had arrived.

The envelope contained ten 8" x 10" glossy black and white promotional pictures. There were two head and three full body shots of Julia Dion in various dance poses.

She was dressed in traditional ballet costumes: tutus and pointe shoes.

She looked to be in her early twenties and very attractive. It was easy to see why St. Jacques wanted to bed her.

According to the brief bio on the back of one of the photos, she had been dancing since her preteens and appeared in a number of productions. She also had two credits as a prima ballerina.. I noticed that she'd danced in three of St. Jacques' productions over the last sixteen months.

Time for another visit to Smithson's studio. Besides, I hadn't spoken with Adele for a day now and she was still paying me.

But first, I needed to call Ernie Coles.

"Coles," he said.

"It's me, Murph," I said.

"Whazzup?"

"Just calling to tell you that you and your crew can pack it in."

"Caught the bastard?"

"Not yet, but closing in. I think the heat is off the girl now and the studio."

"Okay. We'll finish out the day, if that works for you."

"Yeah, fine. Work up your bill and drop it off. I'll have your cash within twenty-four hours, if that's okay with you."

"Yeah, that works. 'Sides, I know you're good for it."

"Great, and thanks for everything, Ernie. By the way, how much you going to charge?"

He gave me a number which I jotted down. It was reasonable and pretty much what I was expecting. I would get a check from Smithson and put it in the bank before the end of the day.

"I'll call you tomorrow and set up a time to meet and settle up."

"Cool. Later," he said, then was gone.

I arrived at the studio around eleven-twenty. It looked like all the classes were in full swing and the main room had a dozen or so dancers going through various maneuvers. I spotted Monique dancing with a young man in the front.

"Mr. Murphy," Adele Smithson said from behind me. "Funny, I was thinking of calling you this morning. And here you are."

"Yeah. Sorry about not calling, but I've been tied up with this business that happened to St. Jacques the other night, as well as the latest things that happened around Monique."

"I thought as much, or at least, hoped that you were. Have you found out anything?"

"Yeah, as a matter of fact. Can we go into your office to talk?"

"Oh, sorry, yes, of course."

Once inside, she poured two cups of coffee and then sat down. I took the chair in front of the desk as usual.

"Well, as you may recall from our last talk, I was beginning to think that the events of the past month may not be local in origin.

That the problem might have originated and followed Levesque and St. Jacques from Montreal. It looks like I'm most likely right."

"I'm not sure I follow you."

"I think that is a personal matter involving St. Jacques and his, um, relationship with a dancer he was involved with."

"You said a dancer? Not Monique?"

"That's the way it looks," I said, taking a sip of coffee. "Seems Monique has an alternate inclination, if you follow me," I said.

"Oh. I see. Yes, of course. I have suspected something along those lines lately. She seems to spend a lot of time with one of my other girls."

"Margo Manson."

"My, you have been busy and thorough," she said.

"It wasn't that hard, actually. They aren't making any effort to keep it secret."

"I suppose that's true. So, now what? Is the danger past?"

"As far as I can see, there shouldn't be any more incidents here at the studio. No point. Whoever it is knows that you have taken steps. Besides, if I'm right, then you were never the target."

"But, why then...?"

"I think it was supposed to be an indirect attempt to get at St. Jacques by trying to sabotage his production by scaring Monique off."

"But she didn't scare easily."

"No, she didn't. That's when they raised the stakes by going after him directly."

"So, it's over then? I mean, there won't be any more attempts on my dancers?"

"That'd be my guess, yes. However, both Levesque and St. Jacques may still be targets. Levesque less so, but definitely, St. Jacques. My question to you is, do your investors and backers want me to stay on the case and protect these people? I mean, I've solved the matter behind the so-called, incidents you actually hired me to look into."

"I think I can safely say, yes. At least, continue unless I instruct you otherwise."

"Right. Because the shooting resulted in a death, the police are now involved as well. I'm sure they've been talking with both Levesque and St. Jacques. I know the investigating detective. We've worked together before. Between the two of us, I'm sure we'll be able to keep them safe and catch whoever is behind this."

"Wonderful. By the way, have you spoken with Pierre about Montreal?"

"Yes. He's aware of what I'm doing. So is Monique."

"Ah, and did they offer any ideas that would support your theory?"

"Not much. But I have other sources."

"Okay. Thank you for bringing this to me. You have done a very good job and I see why Saul thought so highly of you. Is there anything else we need to discuss?"

I went quickly through the billing information for the extra manpower and finished by giving her an invoice for the costs. She wrote me a cheque for the full amount plus an additional two hundred dollars to cover my expenses. I thanked her and before leaving, asked if I could speak with Monique for a moment. She said that would be okay.

I stood by the door to the main dance room and waited to catch Monique's eye. When I finally did, I waved her over. I watched as she skipped across the floor towards me. She made skipping look sexy and graceful. I noticed Margo Mason watching us from over Monique's shoulder.

"Hi," she said. She looked a little flushed from the workout. She wore what I had come to recognize as the standard practice attire, skin tight sleeveless top and stretch pants, leg warmers and silk slippers. She had a terrycloth towel draped around her neck.

"Hi," I said back. "Can you spare a few minutes for a couple more questions?"

"Sure. Let's go there and sit," she said, pointing to a bench just down the hall.

"I just have a few questions about a dancer back in Montreal."

"Julia Dion?"

"That's right. What do you know about her and her relationship with St. Jacques?"

"Not a lot," she said, dabbing the towel under her chin.

"Anything at all would be helpful."

"She was actually gone from Gaudet's when I arrived. But there was still talk about the scene that happened between them."

"Go on."

"I did not hear very much about the fight but several of the other dancers did say that the girl was extremely upset about something."

"Do they say what specifically?" I asked.

"As I recall, she claimed to be pregnant, and it was his. He refused to take responsibility and there was talk of an abortion."

I knew most of this part already. What I needed was a better idea of who Julia Dion was.

"What about Dion? Did you ever meet her? Or talk to her?"

"No. Although, I remember a couple of the other dancers commenting on her religious views."

"Why would that come up in a dance studio?"

She shrugged, saying, "I do not know. But, they said she was a very devout Catholic."

"Okay, thanks. I'll let you get back to your dancing; don't want those muscles to cool down too much."

I watched as she stood and trotted across the studio floor to where Margo was going through movements in front of the mirror. I'll never tire of watching these women move.

I left the studio for my car thinking about what Monique told me about Dion's religion. For myself, I wasn't particularly religious, at least not as a practitioner. I was raised in the Catholic church being from Irish stock but, it never took hold of me.

I do remember the church's attitudes on premarital sex, homosexuality and, especially, abortion. Any of those could create some serious feelings of guilt in a real believer. As I got in the car and started the motor, I asked myself if I'd just found a motive for everything that had gone down?

It was time for another quick talk with Gus Ferguson.

Chapter Twenty-Two

When I arrived at the station, I went directly upstairs to the detective squad room. As usual, it was a beehive of activity as it is most of the time during the day shift. I spotted Gus at his usual place behind a desk by the window. Seniority has its advantages.

He wore the same three piece suit he always seems to wear. I think he must've got a deal on a bulk order for the identical suit. His jacket was hanging from the back of his chair with his hat hooked on one of the corners. He, like a lot of the old timers, wore his service Smith and Weston .32 Police Special in a shoulder holster tucked under his left arm rather than in a belt holster.

"Gus," I said, pulling an empty chair from the next desk and sitting down.

"Murph. What brings you to the zoo today?" he said, sitting back.

I quickly gave him the Reader's Digest version of my recent conversations with Levesque and in Montreal.

"Looks like everything that's been happening is directly connected to the shooting the other night involving St. Pierre Jacques and begins in Montreal."

"Looks that way, right enough, but there isn't any hard evidence to go on."

"Yeah, there's that," I said. "I know what I've got so far is circumstantial but solid. All the pieces fit into a picture of a woman out for revenge. And, according to Levesque, Dion is supposed to be this devoted Catholic."

"So? What does that matter? I'm an Anglian, so what?"

"The Catholic church has some very rigid laws, rules, about shacking up outside of marriage and abortion, especially, abortion. I think it's even an excommunicable sin."

"Sound extreme, I agree, but...?"

"It would create a deep feeling of guilt in a real believer to the point of..."

"Murder," he said, finishing my thought. "Jesus."

'Anyway, I have also learned that no one seems to recall seeing Dion in Montreal for a while. My guess is she's here in the city."

"Don't suppose you have any idea where?"

I shook my head.

"Wait a sec," I said. Can you get in touch with the drug boys and find out if they've got anybody embedded at Rochdale? I'd go in myself, but I'd stand out too much and don't need the hassle with the bikers."

"Good point. So, you think she could hidin' there?"

"Makes sense," I said. "Think about it. You're new to this city with no contacts but

want to be near enough to places where there
are dance studios and an arts community.
But you don't want it widely known you're
here, where could you go, stay?"

"A place where you would blend right in.
Hide in plain sight."

"Bingo."

"I'll make a call," he said. "By the way,
you got a description of the girl?"

"Better. Gaudet's studio sent me
pictures, here's a couple of copies."

I fished out the photos and passed them
over.

"Good looking woman," he said, more to
himself than me as he eyed the images.

"Yeah. I'm hoping to find someone who's
seen her around the Village. It's a tight
community and I have people looking."

"Let me guess, Gabe?"

"Uh-huh. He's plugged into the arts
community."

"No pun intended," Gus said, with a
chuckle.

"Hey, be nice. Gabe's okay."

"Whoa," he said, throwing up his hands.
"No offense meant."

"None taken. But, yeah, he does have a
special relationship with a number of people
from several areas. And he likes me."

"What's not to like," he said, with a hint
of sarcasm which I ignored.

"By the way, how're you making out with
Pete's murder investigation?" I asked.

"We've been trying to track down these kids you told us about. No luck. We've been lookin' in Yorkville and on up in the downtown area checkin' the schools and pool halls. Nothin'. Nobody's seen them or knows anything about them. You?"

"I'm working an angle that might draw them out."

"Care to share?"

"The less you know about the how, the better for the case. What you don't know you can't tell," I said.

"Right. Abe know 'bout this?"

"Uh-huh," I said, nodding.

"And he's cool with it?"

"With what?"

"Right."

Chapter Twenty-Three

I decided to take a run over to Ed's Pool Hall for a quick check in with him. It wasn't that far, and the weather was great, so I opted to walk and enjoy the sunshine. Sometimes I just like to get out and be part of the street life of the Village. Reminds of why I live here.

However, lately, I have started seeing changes in many of the old familiar places and in the people. The Village has long resisted the waves of change that have overtaken many of the boroughs of Toronto, but lately, it seemed that cracks were appearing in the barriers. Familiar faces looked older. Cafe and club venues were moving with the times: less avant-garde; more trendy. The music scene was becoming more eclectic. The hippies seemed diminished somehow; replaced with a new movement comprised of a younger generation. One not so much interested in the artistic or intellectual culture of the Village. You could almost feel it. Like a low pressure system just before a storm. And it wasn't just in Yorkville. It seemed like whatever was coming would wash over the whole country. Something was coming. Something that would redefine everything.

I thought about Pete's death; Elmore giving up the life and becoming a citizen and me married. It all seemed like omens. Time was creeping up and about to overtake me.

By the time I got to Ed's place, I was feeling old. Dated. Bordering on obsolescence.

When Ed saw me, he raised an empty glass. I nodded and took a stool at the bar. He poured out a cold beer from the tap and sat it down in front of me. I couldn't help looking in the corner where Pete always sat, cue in hand.

"You look like you're lower than a snake's belly," Ed said.

"Huh? Oh, yeah. Just remembering," I said.

"Yeah," he said, looking at the empty chair at the end of the pool table. "I'm thinking of taking that table out. Put a couple small tables and chairs in or maybe make it a bandstand or somethin'." Another omen?

"Heard anything yet?" I asked, taking a long pull on my drink. It felt good going down. Cold.

"Yeah. A little. Looks like we wuz right in thinkin' dey were from one a dem schools, ya know, private."

"Anyway, your guy can find out for sure and which one?"

"Already doin' it."

"What about our plan to lure them out?" I finished off my beer.

"You bet. Another?"

"Yeah, why not," I said, reaching for my wallet.

"Forget that. Your money's no good here anymore," he said, as he pulled the tap.

"Thanks."

"We put da word 'round da locals where most a' the shooters play. We did get a nibble from da Derby dat someone was by checkin'."

"Yeah, I heard," I said as he set the glass down. "I think it's time to ramp up the heat. Get the word out that this shooter's heard about this kid and is telling people he wants a game."

"Might work," Ed said, scratching his cheek.

"I figure the kid's ego won't let that slide. In fact, let it be known that he can set the time and place for a match."

"It'll be on da street before dark."

I finished up and left. I had time, so I headed over to see Gabe and give him one of the photographs of Dion. He wasn't in so, I left a note written on the envelope containing the picture and left it with the bartender.

It was getting late, but I wanted to stop by the office, check my mail and collect any messages. When I got back to the office, I found a note someone had slipped under the door. I went and sat down at the desk and opened the sealed letter size envelope. There were no markings on the outside. I detected a faint scent of perfume. Inside was a single sheet of ordinary stationary. The note was handwritten in ink. The flow of the letters suggested it might've been written by a woman. It had that kind of preciseness to the penmanship.

Stay away from St. Jacques, or else.

Cryptic. Direct. I guess there was no mistaking it now, they knew who I was and that I was looking for them. I wondered if it was possibly the shooter who wrote the note. I still had to consider that it might be two of them in this. I guess they figured I was getting too close to them. Glad someone thought so.

I'd have to be careful. If they were prepared to come out of the shadows and threaten me off the trail, then they were prepared to act on it. After all, they already demonstrated a willingness to kill.

I got up and went to the locked wall space where I kept my guns. I pulled out my .22 six shot pistol and shoulder holster and slipped it on, hoping it wouldn't be necessary to use it again as the image of Lucy Addams returned.

I couldn't let that memory interfere with the business at hand, or I might become a statistic. I shook the memory loose, reached inside and picked up the box of ammo. I opened it and took out six rounds and put them in my pants pocket. I was ready.

The phone rang just as I was about to call it a day. It was long distance. Montreal.

"Murphy," I said, picking up.

"This is the long distance operator. I have a collect call from Kevin Jameson. Do you accept?"

"Yes," I said.

"Go ahead with your call," she said in the standard phone company monotone.

"Mr. Murphy? This is Kevin Jameson at Gaudet's. I'm calling with that information you asked for."

"Great. Shoot."

"It looks like Julia has been seen back here in the city."

"When?"

"Two days ago. However, I believe she may also have left again."

"Thanks for letting me know and for the photos."

"Happy to help," he said. "I may not particularly like the man but, as far as his choreography goes he's..."

"A genius," I said, cutting him off. "I've heard. Just so you know, steps have been taken to ensure his safety while he's here."

"That's good to hear. Thank you. Well, good luck Mr. Murphy."

"Thanks." I returned the phone to its cradle.

* * *

The next day I headed back to Pierre St. Jacques' place. I called ahead from home before leaving. There was no answer. I called the front desk operator, and she said that as far as she knew, St. Jacques was still in. He had requested a nine o'clock wake up call. I looked at my watch: eight-thirty. I could be there by nine if I took the car; traffic permitting. I dropped Jane at the library and kissed her good-bye then headed for St. Jacques' hotel.

It was nine fifteen when I had parked the car on a side street about a block away from his hotel and walked the short distance to his building. The doorman on duty said that St. Jacques was still in. I took the elevator to his floor. When I reached his suite I knocked on the door.

"Une moment," St. Jacques called from inside.

"Mr. Murphy," he said, when he opened the door. Good morning. Please," he said, inviting in.

"I was about to have breakfast. Please, come. Sit. Coffee? it is a delicious blend."

"Yeah. Thanks," I said. "Black."

"And why this call on me so early in the day?" he asked, turning his attention back to me.

"I believe I've finally worked out the reason for the attacks and who the person is behind it all. I also believe it's the same person who shot you."

He looked at me over the rim of his cup with a surprised look on his face.

"Who?"

"Julia Dion."

He slowly lowered his cup.

"Impossible!" he said, sounding a bit startled at the idea.

"Everything that's come to light recently suggests otherwise, including the distinct possibility that she is here, in Toronto."

"But why? Why would she do this? It was only a casual liaison."

"I don't know why she would take it in any particular way since we ended our time together before Monique and I became involved."

"You sure about that?"

"Of course. Why would you think it would be otherwise? Mon Dieu, what kind of person do you think she is?"

"She's a woman. They tend to react badly when they think they've been mistreated or taken advantage of sexually or jilted."

"God, how bourgeois," he said, shaking his head.

"Maybe so, but it's a fact nonetheless."

"And you think that she's feeling betrayed? Nonsense."

"It's something to consider," I said. "By the way, did you say that it was you who ended the, uh, affair?"

"Yes."

"When did she tell you she was pregnant?"

"Shortly after I ended our affair. Julia came to me and said she was pregnant and demanded to know what I would do. I said that it was most regrettable but, I did not wish to be a parent at this time and suggested she deal with it."

"Jesus, that was cold," I couldn't help saying. I was really beginning to dislike this man. "And then what?"

"I left. I assume she took care of it."

"By take of it, you mean she had an abortion?"

"I assume so, yes."

"And you think that she would just move on and get over this?"

"It is of no concern to me. I have, as you say, moved on. Why?"

I felt the anger rising in me. It was time to get out of there before I did something I would regret. I had what I came for and more that I didn't want.

"As near as I've been able to put together from the information I've gathered, this liaison, as you call it, may have been much more to her than you. She may be feeling betrayed. Then there's the pregnancy and abortion. Did you know she was a devout Catholic?"

"No. It never came up, why would it?" he said. "Why would that matter?"

"Well, you probably aren't aware of her church's position on premarital sex and, especially, abortion. In case you don't know; the first is a forgivable sin, however, the other is considered serious enough to warrant possible excommunication. This would mean that she would consider her eternal soul condemned forever."

He just sat there staring at me, looking perplexed.

"I...do not understand what this means to me?" he said.

"If she's a devout believer and thinks she has sinned to the point where her church would expel her, it's very likely she would blame you and want to seek revenge for taking away two things she would hold most sacred; her unborn child and her church."

"Mon Dieu, she is mad; insane."

"I don't know about that, but she is definitely off the rails," I said. I finished off the cup of coffee and set it back on the table.

"What must I do?"

My first inclination was to say he should pack his bags and get out of town or the country but, I bit my tongue. "If you plan on staying here, I would advise getting protection, at least until she's found. And maybe stay away from anymore, uh, liaisons until this over."

He shot me a quick nasty look at the last bit but didn't say anything.

"Well, that's all I came here to tellyou so, I'll be on my way. Here's the phone number of someone you can call if wish to hire someone. He's a good man and an ex-cop."

I gave him Ernie Coles' number.

He sank back into his chair looking like a man whose past actions had finally caught up to him, looking for payment, which, of course was the case.

I stopped by the office and saw the message light blinking on the answering machine. There was only one message from Ed. It was still too early to call Ed back so I dialed Ernie Coles number. He was in. I filled him in on the meeting I just had with St. Jacques and my recommending that the man contact him for some protection work. Then I called Gus Ferguson.

"Ferguson," Gus said, when he picked up.

"It's me, Murph," I said.

"Uh-huh. What's up?"

"I just left a meeting with St. Jacques at his hotel. I put him the picture regarding the Dion woman and suggested he get himself some protection. I put him onto Ernie."

"Coles?"

"Uh-huh."

"He's a good man. Too bad he quit the job so early. Anythin' else?"

"Yeah. I got a call from that fella at the Gaudet studio in Montreal. He told me he heard Dion was back in the city. Apparently, she turned up there a day after St. Jacques was shot. However, he did say that he believes she's come back here. Before you ask, he didn't say anything about why she was back there. By the way, any cheer on finding out if the drug squad has a man inside Rochdale?"

"Yeah," he said. "They got two people: a man and a woman. I asked if they'd help us out and they said yes. I sent the photo over to them. If she's holed up there they should be able to find her."

"So, it's a waiting game then?"

"Yeah. You makin' any headway on Pete's killing?"

"Yeah. I think I'll have something for you in a day or two. One of Ed's contacts pigeon-holed me to say some kid has been asking around about the dummy hustler we set up. We've upped the ante on the scam and think this kid'll be in touch very soon."

"Right. Be careful. Remember, he doesn't run alone."

"Not to worry," I said. "When the meet is set, I'll be there with Elmore."

Gus knew about Elmore and my friendship with him. Like Abe, he didn't approve of my friends with highly 'questionable' pasts.

"I hear he's gone straight?"

"Appears so," I said, "at least, that's what T told me."

"Yeah, well, we'll see. Keep in touch, we'll be waitin' on your call."

Ten minutes later, the phone rang.

"Murph."

"Hey, it's me," Ernie said. "Everything's set up with St. Jacques. He's agreed to a three man team. Thanks for referral."

"No sweat. Give me a discount next time I need you."

"You got it, buddy. Thanks again."

"Listen, can you meet me, say in an hour? I'll stand you lunch."

"Yeah, sure. Whazzup?"

"I got your money."

"Cool. Twelve o'clock," he said, then was gone.

That was typical Ernie. An economy of words but a surplus of moxie and balls. He once told me, what he did said more than what he could ever say. I believed him. So did a couple guys now resting in the ground in some out of the way cemetery.

I called Ed last.

"Ed's," he said when he answered in his usual gruff voice. Smoked way too much.

"It's me. Whaddya got?"

"Murph. Yeah, look, I gotta call late last night from 'Three Finger Freddie'. He was over in Little Italy. Anyway, some punks come lookin' fer a game a pool. Dey don't know da place belongs to Mickey Pesci. Anyway, 'cordin' to Freddie, one a 'em lost t'ree straight at a c-note per then tried to welch. Sez, when dey tried ta split, a fella blocked da door. One a' the kids pulled a gun. Next t'ing two a' the kids got popped. Picked the wrong place an' wrong guy."

"Sound like it was it our guys?"

"Looks that way, yeah?"

"What the hell were they thinking for Chrissake trying to pull their shit down there?"

"Beats me," Ed said. "Anyway, looks like it's done."

"So, they're dead then?"

"That's what Freddie t'ought. Everybody sorta hoofed it before da cops show up. Last t'ing he saw was an ambulance pull up."

"What about the third kid? You said that there were three of them the night they jumped Pete."

"Don't know. Freddie only said two. Does it matter? Least they got the one that did him, right?"

"Yeah, I guess so," I said. But a part of me wanted the third kid. It bothered me that one of the bastards would skate on his part in doing Pete in.

"Okay, Ed, thanks for the call."

"Feel good, Murph. Least it's done now an' the prick got his no matter how."

"Yeah. See ya," I said and hung up.

I sat there thinking and after ten minutes or so, I made a decision: I wanted the third kid, and I knew how to do it.

Chapter Twenty-Four

It was a nice day, so I headed out for a quick lunch. I ordered my usual; smoked meat on rye with hot mustard and brown sauerkraut along with two thick Kosher pickles on the side and a cold beer. I sat outside at one of the sidewalk tables that were coming out now that the weather was warming up. It was a great place to think things over while enjoying the food and the passing scenery of long legs, short skirts, and tantalizing figures. The women seemed younger than I remembered; they weren't younger, I was older.

As I sat there mulling this thought over, I started noticing the changes in the Village again and how it felt like something was slipping away. I realized at that moment how much this place had been a part of my life. Christ.

I paid the bill and returned to the office before I really started to get maudlin.

The first thing I did was call Jane. I needed something to kick me in the butt and get the morbid thoughts out of my head. I wasn't ready to see myself as old. Not yet.

"Hey baby," I said, when she picked up.

"Hey yourself. To what do I owe this unexpected call? Mind you, I'm not complaining."

"Nothing. Just wanted to hear your voice is all," I said.

"Uh-oh. What's up? Something happen?" Jane had a built-in radar and could always tell when I was off kilter.

"Naw, really. Nothing's wrong. Guess I'm just feelin' a bit low."

"Okay. Talk," she said.

I didn't want to talk about how I was feeling now, here on the phone, but I knew she wouldn't let it go. Besides, it sounded too much like feeling sorry for myself. So, I said, "Remember those kids I'm looking for that did Pete? Well, I just heard that two of them may have been shot last night over in Little Italy."

"Oh no. How...?"

"Looks like they tried to run their game in the wrong place and on the wrong people."

"I thought there were three of them," she said. She was quick.

"There was. I guess he either wasn't with them or he got away."

"So, what are you going to do now?"

"Find him."

"Uh-huh. Thought so. I knew you wouldn't be happy thinking this boy might get away with killing your friend."

"You're one smart cookie, you know that?"

"Not so smart. I just know the man I love."

"I don't know what I did in this or any other life to deserve you, but I'm glad I got you," I said.

"Yeah, you do," she said softly.

"Thanks, baby. See you tonight. Love you."

"Love you too," she said then hung up.

I was feeling much better. I realized that as long as she was with me for the ride, then getting old would be just fine.

I picked up the phone and dialed Abe's direct line.

"Goldman."

"Hey buddy," I said.

"Murph. What's up?"

"Stand you a cold one later?"

"Sure, why not. Usual place, say five-thirty.?"

"Okay. See you then. Oh, see if Gus wants to join us if he can tear himself away from his desk. I owe him a couple."

"Now there's a challenge. See ya there, later." Then the line was dead.

The usual place was a small tavern near the station called Benny's. It was a popular place with a lot of the cops from the station for a cold one at the end of their shifts.

I went in and found an empty booth. I signaled the bartender for a beer. When he came over I told him that I was expecting Abe and maybe Gus and asked him to bring a couple of pitchers when they arrived. He nodded and walked back behind the bar. Ten minutes later my two friends walked in.

"Abe. Gus," I said, as they slipped into the booth opposite me. "Glad you could join us, Gus."

"Thanks. Been a while. Figured, what the hell, good day for a cold one," he said, taking off his hat and setting it on the seat between him and Abe.

The bartender arrived with a couple of tall pitchers of beer and two more glasses and set them on the table.

"So? What's up?" Abe asked, as he poured out two glasses and topped mine up.

"Hey, can't a guy just have a beer with a couple of buds?"

"Uh-huh."

"Okay. Yeah, I got a call from Ed, you remember him. Well, he's had a couple of his boys looking out for those kids that did Pete. Turns out the reason we had a hard time locating them was they were from Scarborough. Anyway, seems they showed up again. Tried to run their hustle in Little Italy. Long story short, two got popped late last night."

"Yeah, I heard somethin' this morning when I got in," Gus said. "Report said they were taken to the hospital. Seems both are in serious condition but looks like they'll make it."

"Oh? Interesting. Ed's guy was pretty definite about them being killed," I said.

"What makes Ed so sure it's the same kids that attacked Pete?" Gus asked, picking up his glass and taking a long swig.

"I didn't ask. I figured his guys know who they were," I said. Besides, what're the chances of two kids running hustle with same M.O. as the ones that did Pete happening again at another pool hall?"

"Okay. I'll make a couple of calls," Gus said.

"Is it too much to hope you'll keep me in the loop?"

"Yeah, don't worry. When I find out anything, I'll let you know."

"By the way, you said Ed told you two kids were involved. Wasn't there three before?" Abe asked.

"Uh-huh. I'm hoping you'll be able get something out of one a' the boys in the hospital. I'm thinking he either wasn't there or, if he was, he managed to split. If you can find him and brace him he'll spill on Pete's case and maybe even on who hit his buddies, assuming he was there. One way or the other, he's gotta be pretty scared."

"Good point," Gus said, as he picked up the pitcher and poured another round of top ups..

"How're things going on the dancer case?"

"I think I got enough evidence to lay everything from the so-called accidents to the shooting the other night on a dancer named, Julia Dion." I ran everything I had by them.

"It all sounds pretty circumstantial to me," Abe said when I finished.

"I know but, you hafta admit, it's still pretty solid."

"Yeah, you're right; it does sound that way. Gus is up on everything, so I'll leave it with him," Abe said. "I assume you'll be goin' after her?"

"Yeah," I said nodding. "Once I got her in hand I'll turn her over to Gus."

We sat and chatted over the second pitcher of beer then called it a day and headed out to our respective lives.

The following morning, I got a call from Adele Smithson asking me to come over to the studio. I arrived around ten.

I managed to find a parking spot where I wouldn't be ticketed two blocks away. It was a clear sunny morning so the walk would be fine. The street was busy with traffic and pedestrians going about their daily routines.

When I arrived at the studio everything looked fine: classes were in full swing, and the main room looked busy as well. I did note that Monique and Margo weren't anywhere to be seen. Adele was in her office as usual.

Today she wore a soft pink cashmere sweater and a black knee length skirt with a wide red belt around her waist. The lady was a classy dresser and knew how to cover all her good parts to the best effect.

I saw immediately that she looked distressed when I entered her office.

"Oh, Mr. Murphy. I'm so glad you are here," she said, standing up.

"What's wrong? What happened?" I said, closing the door.

"It's this," she said, picking up a sheet of paper and passing it over to me.

I pulled a chair over, sat down and read the page.

If you don't stop you're next

"What does this mean? Am I in danger? My dancers? The studio?" she asked, sounding like she was on the verge of becoming hysterical.

"Okay, take a deep breath and calm down," I said.

She closed her eyes and sat back in her chair. I watched her chest rise as she pulled in a deep breath of air.

"That's it. Take a couple more. Good. Now tell me, when did you get this?" I asked, once I saw she seemed calmer.

"It was under the door when I opened this morning. I thought this was over."

"Did you call the police?"

"No. Just you. I didn't know what to do. Does this mean they would actually do something to my studio or to me?"

"I don't think so," I said. "It's meant to scare you."

"It's working. I'm terrified," she said.

"That's what whoever is doing this is counting on. I don't think they'll carry through with the threat," I added quickly.

"But if they do, then what? They shot St. Jacques."

I saw the look of fear in her eyes. "Look. The police and I are closing in on them. They got to be feeling the heat so, I doubt that they would chance any move against you at this point. They have to know that your place is probably being watched. It would be too risky for them to expose themselves."

"Well, that may be but right now, I'm scared. I hate this. I don't know what to do."

"First, I want to you call this number and ask for Detective Ferguson. You remember him. When you get him, tell him about the note and that you've called me. Tell him you're afraid for your dancers and the studio and ask for protection. He'll arrange to send over a couple of uniformed cops to watch the place. Okay?"

She nodded.

"Good. Next, I want you to try and relax. I'll take care of this. If it's any comfort, I think I know who's behind this and have initiated a search for her."

"Her?"

"Yes. I'm sure it's the woman from Montreal that St. Jacques was working with as well as sleeping with. By the way, I noticed when I came in, Monique and Margo aren't in today. Know why?"

"I hadn't noticed. I was too upset by this this note. Let me check the schedule. They may not be here today." She opened a large ledger on the desk and slid her finger down the page.

"Yes, here it is. She isn't due in until this afternoon for a rehearsal," she said, looking up from the ledger at me.

I looked at my watch, eleven thirty. I decided to take a quick run over to their apartment and check on them.

"So? You going to be okay now?"

"I'll manage. Thank you for coming over so quickly. I'm not used to any of this, and it scares me silly."

"Most people aren't used to this sort of stuff, Adele. Don't worry, you're stronger than you realize."

"Thank you," she said with a smile.

"Okay then. I'm off. Call Ferguson," I said.

"I will."

I was just about to turn onto the street where the two women lived when I spotted Monique and Margo rounding the corner together. They were both dressed in slacks and light jackets and were carrying big bags slung over their shoulders. They walked along toward the subway entrance at the end of the block chatting and laughing.

The traffic on the street was brisk, so I couldn't stop. I slowed down and tooted my horn but they didn't notice or pay attention. Suddenly there was a loud blast from the air horn of a delivery van behind me. I had slowed down too much and was now causing a problem on the street. It was at that moment that I spotted her. Julia Dion. She had reacted to the horn and turned to look.

She was about half a block behind them. She was dressed in denims and a windbreaker with a hood that she wore up. She had her hands stuffed inside the jacket's pockets. Within a matter of a few seconds, she saw me. She stopped and looked right at me, then turned and hurried off across the street, merging into the pedestrian traffic. I watched her in the rear view mirror until she disappeared into the crowd.

I desperately looked for a place to pull out of traffic and park but couldn't see anything. I could only sit in the car and curse my bad luck. At least, I thought, as I continued on down the Street, Monique was safe; for now.

I got the car turned north again and headed for St. Jacques' hotel. I had to give Ernie Coles a head's up on Dion's presence.

They weren't there when I arrived. I headed to the theater where St. Jacques was supposed to be staging his production.

I found Mal Hudson standing off in the wings backstage. He said everything was cool so far. I filled him in quickly on making Dion and made sure he had seen her picture, telling him to keep a sharp eye open. I also told him that it was looking like she was ramping up her efforts with her threat at the studio and spotting her following Levesque. He told me Ernie was due to come by shortly and he would fill him in. I told him to tell Ernie to put a man back on Levesque and to call me if he had any questions. I left and headed back to the office.

Chapter Twenty-Five

Julia Dion.

She was definitely here and was serious about doing something violent against St. Jacques. It looked like Monique was still in danger, as well as Adele, if what just happened was any indication.

The woman was proving to be more dangerous than I thought. But, I wondered, how was she doing this? Some things were just not adding up. Like, how did she get a gun, assuming she was the shooter at the restaurant? How was she able to stay out of sight? Did she know someone here and if so, was that someone connected somehow?

I needed to check in with Gus again and see if he had heard anything from his contacts in the drug squad. I had a strong feeling that we would find out she was hiding inside Rochdale. It was the only place she could go where she could hide in plain sight.

I needed to get a lot more background on her. A lot more.

As soon as I stepped inside my office, I picked up the phone and dialed Gus' number.

"You'll never guess who I spotted today?" I said when he answered.

"Who?"

"Julia Dion."

"Yeah? Where?"

"Outside the Levesque girl's apartment following her down the street. I got a call from Smithson this morning. Something's happened. When she got in this morning, there was a note left under the door to the studio. A threat. I told her to call you."

"Yeah, I know. She called about an hour ago. I sent a coupla uniforms over. Left about half an hour ago."

"Great. Thanks. Anyway, after I left her, I decided to check on Levesque and drove over to her place. I got there just as she and her partner were headed the subway. I couldn't get to them because I was stuck in the car in traffic. That's when I saw her. It was definitely Julia Dion. She was following them."

"And you couldn't get out of the car?"

"Too much traffic. A transport truck behind me blasted his air horn which caused her to turn around, that's when she spotted me and took off."

"And still no idea where she's holed up?"

"None but, I'm holding out on the idea she's at Rochdale. You hear back from your contacts in the drug squad yet?"

Nothin'," he said.

"Shit. By the way, do you have ideas on where she could've laid her hands on a gun?"

"Maybe. You think she got one here? I woulda thought she brought one with her Montreal."

"Good point," I said. "Still…?"

"Yeah. I'll make some calls."

"Thanks. By the way, any word on the third kid yet?"

"Not yet. I'm waitin' for the hospital to call tellin' me I can talk to the two they got. You know, even when we find him it'll be hard to nail him."

"Wrong. We got someone who can I.D. him as one of the three last seen with Pete."

"Ed," Abe said.

"Ed. I figure, if you can find him and haul him in for questioning say, then Ed tags him, well…" I said.

"Yeah. Maybe," he said. "Might work, if we can scare him enough before he lawyers up."

"That's what I was thinking," I said.

"Okay. Watch your back, buddy. Remember, the Dion chick knows you."

"I know." I hung up, pulled out my gun and popped the cylinder out, checking it had all six rounds loaded.

I headed down to see Gabe. Maybe he had some luck and found something that could help me find Dion.

The traffic was moderate; cars, cabs, buses and trucks everywhere. Even the sidewalks seemed full for the time of day. I managed to find a parking spot not too far from the club where I wouldn't be in danger of a ticket, got out and made my way through the crowd.

"Hey Murph," said one of the waitresses, as she bounced by when I stepped inside.

"Hey doll," I said back.

"The usual?" she asked.

"Yeah. Why not."

I stepped across the floor to the empty booth by the kitchen door. My usual spot.

"Here ya go," she said, placing a tall glass of cold draft in front of me, a moment after I'd settled into the booth.

"Gabe around?"

"In the kitchen. Want him?"

"When he's got a minute. No rush," I said.

"Okay," she said, then slipped away. I watched as she went. Couldn't help myself. She was wearing the latest fad going around: A snug light colored T-shirt and a short skirt. And I do mean short. The hem had to be a full twelve inches above her knees; if you put a buckle on it you could call it a belt. However, she had the legs for it: long, tapered, soft looking.

Whoa. Down boy, I thought, take it home.

"What dirty little thoughts are you thinking I wonder?"

"Huh. Oh, hi Gabe."

He slid into the booth opposite me chuckling.

"Christ, how can you work looking at that all day?" I said, looking back at the girl.

"Uh..." he said.

"Oh, yeah, right. Sorry."

"No apology needed. I do understand, believe me. You know I wasn't always gay."

"Really?"

"Uh-huh. Like a lot of us, we went through what I guess you'd call an experimental period. More because of social and family pressures. But then I realized women weren't my preference."

"I didn't know that," I said. "I'm glad you found what made you happy."

"Finally, yes. But it wasn't an easy road. But that's not what you're here for, is it?"

"No. Any word yet?"

"No, sorry. If your girl is in the Village then she's a ghost. At least, in the areas where I checked. I can't say about the other denizens, I'm afraid."

"That's okay. I've been thinking, since she's a dancer, it would make sense she'd try and find a place in that community. So, I' working on a hunch she might be at..."

"Rochdale," he said, finishing my sentence.

"Uh-huh."

"Makes complete sense to me."

"Yes. But keep your eyes open all the same. You never know, she might trip up."

"Certainly"

"By the way, I got a question for you. You're going to think it's weird."

"Ooo, I like weird," he said, laughing.

"If someone wanted to lay their hands on a gun, would you know where to send them, or who to talk to?"

"A gun? Good God, no."

"I thought not. Just figured I'd ask, since you know pretty much everything that happens here in the Village."

"Thank you for that. I have been around, haven't I?"

"Like some of us, yeah," I said.

"The beer is on the house," he said, then slipped out of the booth.

"Thanks. I'll be in touch."

I called Jane on the way out of the club and told her I'd pick her up. Back on the street, I headed for the car.

Chapter Twenty-Six

Two days later all hell broke loose. It started with a call from Ernie Coles just after lunch.

I had just hung up from a call with Gus who let me know that they found the third kid and had him in custody. Ed came in and identified him as one of the three kids the night of Pete's death. He said the kid cracked like an eggshell within an hour of questioning. Bottom line; he and his friends were charged with manslaughter and accessories to murder and remanded to Juvenile Services pending a court date.

I hung up and a moment later, it rang.

"Murph, it's Ernie. We got a problem," he said when I answered.

"Talk to me," I said.

"St. Jacques and the Levesque woman have been shot. They're on the way to the hospital as we speak. Mal's shot too. Dead."

"What the hell happened, for Chrissake?" I yelled.

"I arrived ten minutes after the shooting to relieve Mal. According to witnesses, St. Jacques and Levesque were coming outta the theater when it happened. Figured they musta been heading for lunch. Anyway, a car pulled up to the curb and your woman jumps out waving a gun. She starts screaming at them in French then shot them. Mal was just a hundred feet away and was runnin' toward them when she turned the gun on him. Looks like she got off a lucky shot. One in the heart. Dead instantly. She got back into the car and took off. Whole thing took less than two minutes. Sorry, man. We blew it."

"Don't worry about it. You did your job. By the way, did Mal have anybody?"

"Yeah. Ex-wife an' three kids. Was still in touch with them."

"Christ," I said.

"Shit happens. He was a good man, and he knew the risks."

"Yeah. They gonna be okay?"

"Shirley? Yeah. She's covered. Got a new husband."

"Okay, good. By the way, any idea which way the car went?"

"Looks like they was headed back to the Village."

"Right. Thanks. Looks like you're done. Make up your bill and get it to me."

"Look, Matt, if it's okay with you, I want to stay in. Mal was my friend."

"Okay."

"Thanks," he said.

"You got any contacts in the Village you can use?"

"I know some people, yeah. Whatcha got in mind?"

"I figure the only place she's likely holed up is Rochdale. The place, as you well know, is a Goddamn zoo. Most people, even the cops, won't go in there unless they absolutely have to."

"They shoulda burned that place down long ago. Bunch a fuckin' freaks in there now; freaks an' them biker assholes."

"Main reason I haven't gone there but, I can't put it off any longer. By the way, did you happen to get anything on the getaway car?"

"Yeah," he said. "Late model Ford, Pinto, I think. Should be easy to make; it's carryin' Quebec plates."

"Right. Let's hook up and take a run up to the college. If I'm right and she's up there, she could be getting ready to make a run for it."

"How ya figure?"

"I think the driver of the car must be her brother. If you're right about which way they took off, she could be going back to get their stuff."

"Makes sense. Okay. I'll be on the sidewalk waitin'."

"Good. I should be there in fifteen minutes. Do me a favour and call Gus Ferguson and fill him in on what happened and my plan."

"No problem." I hung up and headed for the door, telling Maddie to lock up.

I got to my car and headed to the theater. Everything had quieted down by the time I arrived. The cops were still canvassing the area. The emergency vehicles and the Forensic guys were gone. I spotted the chalk outline on the sidewalk which was taped off. I spotted Ernie and tooted my horn. He saw me and dashed across the street and got in.

"All set?" I asked as he settled into the seat.

"Hit it," he said. "I passed everything to Gus. He's sending a coupla squad cars to meet us there."

I pulled away from the curb, squealing my tires.

Coles gave more details on the car as I drove. We worked out a plan of action if the cops weren't there by the time we arrived.

"Ya know they might not come easy?" he said as pulled out his revolver.

"Yeah," I said. "I know."

"Jus' sayin'."

I concentrated on the road as I maneuvered through the traffic. We finally reached Bloor Street West and I made a left turn onto it. Rochdale College was a couple of blocks down on the left side of the road. We could see it in the distance. There were sixteen stories above a high main floor area that housed a small restaurant in a corner of the building. Each floor had a row of windows on it, looking a lot like most of the downtown office towers. As usual, there were fifty or more people milling about the main entrance. Motor bikes and hogs were parked on the street and the open quad in front of the building. We didn't see any squad cars.

"Cruise 'round the buildin', see if they parked on the street," Ernie said, leaning forward and staring out the windscreen. "Maybe take a turn down Huron."

"Yeah, good idea," I said as I neared the corner of Huron Street.

We got lucky.

"There," he said, pointing to a red Fort Pinto with Quebec plates parked about a quarter of the way down the street. "That's the car. I sure of it. Now what?"

I spotted a vacant opening four cars ahead and slowly pulled into it.

"I caught a break," I said, shutting off the engine. "I was really hoping we wouldn't have to go inside the building. Now we got a chance to take them outside, away from the civilians, in case they opt to go hard." I sounded like cop. Some of the old training still sneaked through.

"Works for me. How ya wanna play it?"

"I figure one on each side of the street. One to cut them off from pulling out if they make into the car; the other to have either side of the car in case they make a run for the doors."

"Yeah, that'd work alright. Which do you want?" he asked.

"Don't much matter. I guess I'll take this side of the street. You take up a position over there in the alley between the blue an' green houses. That'd give you a good sight line on the front of the car from between the two parked cars there," I said, pointing. "I'll take up my position behind that Chevy behind their car. We'll take them when they reach their car."

"Right. Good luck," he said then headed for the alley.

A few minutes later, I heard the sound of sirens in the distance. Dion and a young man I assumed was her brother came running down the street towards their car. They each had a bag in hand.

I pulled out my gun and stood up, bending slightly over the trunk of the Chevy.

"Julia Dion," I yelled out, showing my head above the roof of the car when they reached their car. "Drop the bag and put your hands where I can see them." I still didn't show my weapon.

She reacted swiftly by dropping the bag and pulling her other hand out of her coat pocket with a gun in it.

Suddenly, time seemed to stop as she raised her arm at the same moment I saw Ernie step into the street with his gun up yelling at her to drop it while her brother was reaching an arm across the hood of the car calling out her name. Then Ernie fired. The sound shattered the moment, and everything came back to normal.

His shot caught her in the shoulder, spinning her around like a rag doll, throwing her gun arm up as she fired. The shot going wild.

Everything was over in less than a minute.

When I stepped out from behind the Chevy and reached her, she was lying in her brother's arms. He was weeping.

Epilogue

The case was over. Gus Ferguson had arrived and taken Julia and her brother into custody. She was formally charged with murder and assault with a deadly weapon, while her brother was charged as an accessory and the procurement and possession of an illegal firearm for the purpose of committing a felony.

I arranged a meeting with the Crown Attorney's office where I surrendered all the information I had obtained on the circumstances behind her actions in the hope that it would help her. Our courts are tough but also fair. At least I had to believe they were.

Three days later, Jane and I were taking advantage of another gorgeous day of sunshine and gentle breezes, taking in the sights and entertainments of Yorkville. We sauntered by the various shops, looking at pieces of artwork and handicrafts being offered. We even purchased a couple of items for the apartment.

"What do you think will happen to her now?"

"I talked with the one of the attorneys after I gave all the background information I had on the case. He said his office might consider going for diminished capacity or something like that, or at least I hope so. There's certainly enough extenuating circumstances."

"Well, I'm happy it's over and it ended the way it did. One ghost in your life is enough."

"Amen to that," I said.

We decided to find a cafe with sidewalk tables where we could get a light lunch.

"Having fun?" I asked, as we looked over the small menu.

"Mmmm, yes. This was a wonderful idea."

I looked at her for several moments while she read.

"You're doing it again," she said, without looking up.

"Huh? What?"

"Ha, ha, you know damn well what."

"Can't help it. You look different today."

"Different? How?"

"I can't quite put my finger on it but...there's something."

"Some detective you are," she said with a soft chuckle.

"So, there is something?"

"Uh-huh."

"Well. You gonna spill the beans or what?"

"How would you feel about moving to a larger apartment?"

"Huh?" Brilliant or what. "A larger apartment? Why? What's wrong with what we have?"

"We need another bedroom."

"Another bed..." Then the light came on in a blinding flash.

"You mean, you're...?"

"Uh-huh," she nodded. "It's okay, right?"

"It's more than okay. When did you know?"

"Last week. I went to the hospital, and they ran the tests. Everything came back fine," she said smiling. "You're sure you're okay with this?"

"More than you know, baby. More than you know." I got up and went over and took her in my arms.

The End

H. Paul Doucette has lived and worked in many countries throughout a varied career in International Transportation ranging from twelve years as a merchant seaman to a career as an industrial logistic specialist.

He spent a few years 'thumbing' his way across North America and Mexico during the cultural revolution of the sixties and early seventies, during which time he participated in the civil rights and antiwar movements of the time.

He has also enjoyed moderate success as a Fine Art Black and White Photographer. Now he is pursuing his interest as a writer of period set mysteries.

In addition to the Robichaud Mystery series he has also written two other series; one set in Greenwich Village in the 1960s and another war time series set in the Pacific.

He has been retired for more than twenty years and lives in Dartmouth, Nova Scotia.

9 780228 627623